# Fearless Love

## Kate Kadence

CRIMSON
ROMANCE

F+W Media, Inc.

Published by
Crimson Romance
an imprint of F+W Media, Inc.
10151 Carver Road, Suite 200
Blue Ash, OH 45242. U.S.A.
*www.crimsonromance.com*

ISBN 10: 1-4405-8266-1
ISBN 13: 978-1-4405-8266-0
eISBN 10: 1-4405-8267-X
eISBN 13: 978-1-4405-8267-7

This is a work of fiction. Names, characters, corporations, institutions, organizations, events, or locales in this novel are either the product of the author's imagination or, if real, used fictitiously. The resemblance of any character to actual persons (living or dead) is entirely coincidental.

Cover art © 123RF/Syda Productions and iStockphoto.com/mythja

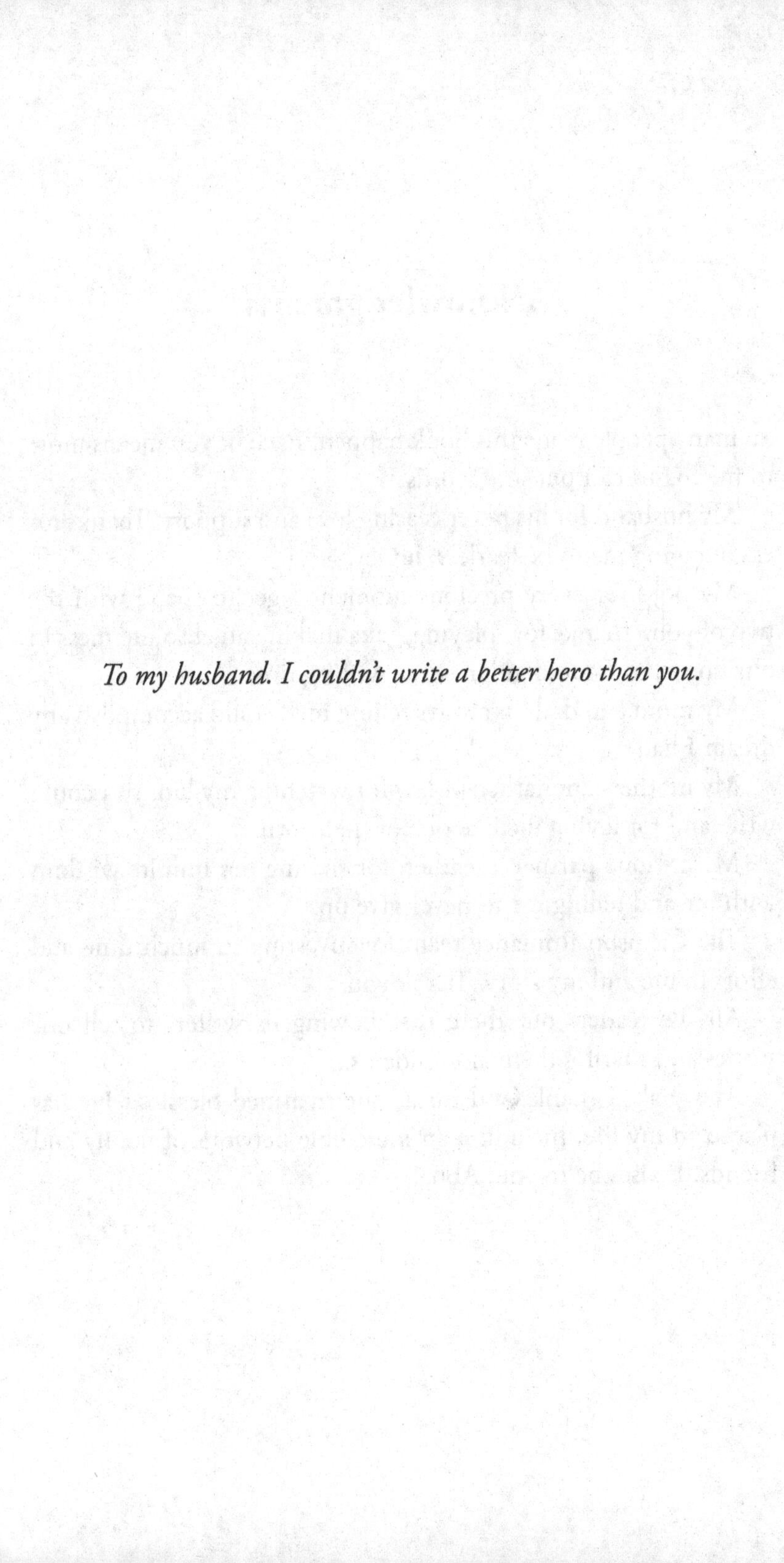

*To my husband. I couldn't write a better hero than you.*

# Acknowledgments

So many people made this book happen. Each of you means more to me than I can put into words…

My husband for his never ceasing love and support. Thanks for encouraging me to be fearless, honey.

My boys for every precious moment I get to spend with the two of you. Thanks for "playing," aka making an absolute mess in our house, so I could get in some writing time.

My mom and dad for always telling me I could accomplish any dream I had.

My mother- and father-in-law for watching my kids so I could write and for loving me like one of their own.

My critique partner, Heather, for sharing her infinite wisdom with me and telling me to never give up.

The Crimson Romance team for investing so much time and effort in me and my story. Thank you.

All the readers out there for allowing us writers to tell our stories and sharing them alongside us.

Above all, I thank God for all the treasured blessings He has placed in my life, including an incredible network of family and friends. Praises be to you, Abba!

# CHAPTER ONE

The shot would have been perfect if not for the helicopter landing in the middle of it.

Madison Carmichael had her finger poised on her Canon 5D Mark II camera, ready to take the photo that would seal the deal on the Addison-Temple wedding contract when instead she heard the deafening sound of the demise of her dream. It started off like a thumping buzz in her ear, but morphed into pounding thunder as the helicopter circled above, sending the California oak trees surrounding them into a feral flurry and her engaged couple fleeing the scene. What crazy person landed in the middle of a field on private property, in Serenity Creek no less?

Her photography business was on the brink of going under and her biggest client, the one who had the referral clout to get her into the market and the money to stabilize her finances, couldn't escape fast enough.

She let her camera hang around her neck and curled her hands into fists at her side. She hadn't worked this hard for five years to stop now. She would pull herself out of this, but first she needed to have a little chat with the hotshot pilot.

She stormed toward the grounded helicopter, its blades almost stopped now. Maybe there was a logical explanation for a helicopter setting down on her parents' property. She knew nothing about flying objects and didn't really care for them—maybe something was wrong.

The door opened and a tall, well-built man jumped down. From this distance, he looked fine and healthy, which kindled her temper.

The odor of gas and engine warred with the wildflowers crushed under the landing gear. She walked straight up to his backside, determined to give him a large piece of her mind. Who did this guy think he was?

"Listen, pal."

He turned around at the sound of her voice and her step faltered.

The man was gorgeous. Dark, almost black, hair tousled by the airstream of the slowing helicopter blades gave him a sexy, rugged appearance. Deep blue eyes roamed her body, starting at her toes and inching their way up to her thoroughly tangled hair.

She could feel the sweat sliding down her neck from the late summer heat. She cleared her throat, tucking her hair behind her ear as if that would calm her tousled locks.

There was definitely nothing wrong with the man in front of her. Setting her hands on her hips, she put all of her wrath into the glare she sent him. "Are you all right?"

The man raised his eyebrows. "Yes."

"Then what makes you think you can just land anywhere you like? This is private property."

The corner of his mouth quirked up in a half smile that set her heart racing. She couldn't tell if anger or desire made her heart pound, but she hoped it was the former. The guy just blew her biggest career opportunity.

"I'm sorry, I don't think we've met. I'm Jake Colt."

He said the words as if she should recognize the name, but the only thing she noticed was the sidestep he took around her question.

"Madison Carmichael." She shook his hand. He brushed his thumb ever so slightly over the back of her hand the instant before she broke off the handshake. "That's my family's winery, Oak Hills, over there and this is still their property. What makes you think you can land here for the fun of it? You just lost me my largest client. Do you have any idea how long it took me to get that chance with them?"

He cocked his head to the side, a puzzled expression on his face. "Sorry, but I'm not quite sure how my landing here lost you your client."

She opened her mouth, but shut it again. She couldn't answer him when she didn't know herself how a bridezilla had blamed her for the helicopter incident. "That doesn't matter, what matters is that you did." That was a solid argument if she'd ever heard one. What happened to her composure?

He chuckled, actually chuckled. "Okay, well I apologize for the mishap. I'll compensate you for whatever money you would have earned," he paused, his eyes settling on the camera around her neck, "photographing them. I assume a check will suffice."

Her mouth fell open. "Are you serious? Money doesn't solve everything."

His expression turned hard. "Neither do pride and stubbornness. I'm being more than fair considering I've done nothing wrong."

"Nothing wrong? You've done everything wrong and I don't need your help."

"Everyone needs help sometimes."

She felt more naked now with his words than she had when he'd undressed her with his eyes. "Sounds a little silly coming from the guy with his own helicopter who sets down wherever he pleases."

"I have every right to land here." His deep, rich voice rose an octave.

"You're delusional. Stop talking like you own the place and everything around it." She took a solid stride forward, ready to tell him to fly right back out of here, when Cork, her family's black Lab, come bounding up to them, tail wagging.

The dog ran straight past her and right up to Jake. Traitor.

"Hey, buddy." He knelt down to the dog, patting his head and scratching his belly as Cork rolled onto his back. "What's your name, huh? You're a sweet one."

She ground her foot into the dirt, taking several deep breaths to rein herself in. Normally, she had such a good grasp on her emotions and could think on her feet when everything fell apart. She needed those skills to be a wedding photographer when passions ran amuck and her job consisted of capturing every special moment, planned and unplanned. But this crazy incident marked the end of a bad week and spelled certain disaster for her business, so politeness could take a day off, especially with Jake "It's All About Me" Colt in front of her.

"Must not be your dog." He glanced up at her. "Too nice."

"That's it." She put her hands up in a stopping motion. "Get off my property. Take your idiotic flying contraption and leave."

He stood slowly, still rubbing Cork behind the ear and stared at her in silence for a split second. "No."

"What?"

"I said no. It's not your property."

She huffed. "Fine. Get off my parents' property. Does that spell it out better for you?"

"It's not your parents' property either."

The guy had to be crazy. "Excuse me?"

"It's my property."

"You're nuts. Get that helicopter out of here and stay away from me. Come on, Cork."

Cork glanced up at Jake and whimpered.

She clenched her teeth. "Cork, right now. Heel."

The dog trudged next to her, turning his gaze back to Jake every few steps. She sent one last seething stare at the eccentric, bizarre, gorgeous stranger before stomping through the field to her childhood house.

She hesitated and looked over her shoulder. He stood there, watching her leave before sending her a quick salute and going back to rummage in the cockpit for who knew what.

The nerve of the guy. Where did he get off thinking he owned the place? And that he could buy his way out of his selfish actions?

"What an egotistical jerk," she told Cork. "And you snuggled right up to him."

She might need money, but she didn't need his help. She would make it on her own like the rest of her family. Something Jake Colt probably couldn't understand.

She pulled her cell phone out of her pocket to call her father. She heard his familiar voicemail message.

"Dad, you're never going to believe what happened. Some nut job just parked his helicopter in your field behind the vineyards. Call me ASAP."

Cork ran for the porch as they reached the white picket fence separating the buttercream and white trim Victorian farmhouse from their vineyard. She threw open the small wooden gate with enough force to send it banging closed behind her with a loud crack.

She had to put a cap on her anger. Friday night meant family dinner, and her foul mood wouldn't be welcome. But she couldn't shake it. Who was that man and what was he doing here?

The delicious scent of freshly baked apple pie assailed her as she walked through the back door into the informal kitchen filled with knickknacks she and her brother had made throughout their school years. It almost soothed the aggravation pounding in Madison's head. Almost.

"You won't believe what is sitting in your field right now." Madison took care to set her camera in a safe spot behind the pie, against the white-tiled backsplash.

She reached for a sweet sample before Rose Carmichael swatted her hand.

"No taste testing," Rose scolded. "And whatever's in the field I'm sure is fine. Don't worry about it." She waved her hand in the air, dismissing the topic.

Not the response she had expected. Peace and calm always surrounded her mother, but wasn't she the least bit interested?

"Don't worry about it? But there's a … "

"Madison, this is an important night for us and, right now, I just need your help with what's happening in here, not outside."

Her mother gave her a stern look, but the pleading in her eyes made her stomach drop. Whatever surprise she and her father wanted to announce tonight must be big and nothing good considering Mom just used her real name instead of her usual endearment.

Opting for a more subtle approach, she stood over the delicacy, breathing in its tangy scent. "Mmm. I love it when you make your famous apple pie."

"That's why I made it. Adam appreciates it, too. He should be here soon." Rose spared the clock a quick glance before putting the finishing touches on her lasagna.

There wasn't much she and her brother didn't like. Rose's cooking could make a restaurant famous, something Adam had tried many a time with his own restaurant. But Rose refused to cook for anyone except her family and friends, which by her way of thinking meant the entire town, so a restaurant shouldn't have been too much of a strain.

Rose picked up the lasagna, struggling under the weight of it. She turned toward the oven and bumped into the corner of the kitchen island, sending the dish tipping precariously to one side.

Madison rushed to grab it before it clattered to the floor.

"Here, let me get this for you." She took the huge lasagna from her mother, carrying it over to the double ovens.

"Thank you, dear." Rose went to the fridge to pull out ingredients for a garden salad.

Madison juggled the dish while opening the oven door and slid it in.

"Are you feeding an army tonight? That lasagna is huge." Madison hooked her thumb over her shoulder.

"Oh, you never know who might be coming to dinner." Rose shrugged her shoulders, bending further over the salad bowl.

Something about her tone set Madison on edge. "Mom, I know you're always hoping Adam and I will bring dates to Friday night dinner but, neither one of us is in a relationship right now. There isn't anyone to bring home or anywhere else for that matter. Believe me, I wish there were, but the pickings are pretty slim around here, and I want to focus on getting into wedding photography. With all the people getting married close to here, the work would be so much steadier than the mishmash of jobs I'm able to scrounge up now."

She blew out her breath and started chopping the tomato her mother handed her. Talk about adding to her irritation level for the day. Dwelling on the fact that she hadn't had a relationship beyond a few dates since she and Tucker White had crashed and burned would do nothing to ease her sour mood.

"That's not what I meant."

Madison waited for her to expand, but her mother said nothing more as she cut up carrots. She took a breath to broach the topic of the helicopter again, but Rose cut her off.

"Are your clients joining us for dinner? They looked like such a nice couple."

Madison halted mid-slice, the muscles in her shoulders tightening. "No. No, they won't be joining us anytime soon."

She couldn't tell her mother they had fired her. It would be admitting she once again had failed in getting her business off the ground. She could barely get it to taxi the runway, considering the length of time that stretched between her paychecks.

Rose dropped the chopped carrots into the bowl and turned toward her. "You know your dad and I are owed some favors. Mrs.

Tuttle's daughter is getting married next year; I'm sure I could get her to hire you."

Madison shook her head. "Not a chance. I want to earn my business, not have it handed to me out of pity."

Rose sighed. "Sweetie, you're investing too much of yourself into your photography. I know it's important to you, but love and family are more essential than any business."

"Mom, you couldn't possibly understand. You and dad built your dream. You're living it."

"We might understand more than you think."

She'd never seen her mom so cryptic. Did she already know a helicopter sat in her backyard? Somehow the thought disturbed her even more than the incident itself.

Rose touched her arm. "Are you okay? You seem a little stressed."

That was a laughable understatement. She couldn't put it off any longer; her mom had to listen this time. "The photo shoot was interrupted."

"Oh no, what happened? Did the bride and groom get called away?"

"Nothing that simple. Some moron landed a helicopter in the middle of the shot. That's what's in your field right now. Can you believe it? A helicopter."

Some of the color left Rose's cheeks. "Oh, I, uh … "

"I mean he landed there like he owned the place." Her speech escalated, as did the speed with which she cut up a cucumber. "He was so arrogant."

"You saw him?"

"Of course I saw him. I walked right up to him to tell him what I thought of his little stunt. He imagined himself so smooth and handsome."

"What did you tell him?"

Madison grabbed another cucumber even though the salad had been saturated with them.

"What? Oh, I don't know, something about him needing to get off our property and who did he think he was for landing here in the first place. I mean the handsome part might be true, but he's not that good-looking." He was, but the best way to convince herself he wasn't would be to keep repeating it.

And now the floodgates had been opened and she couldn't close them against the pounding river of her frustration. "He actually had the nerve to say he owned the place and he offered me money. I mean, really. Money."

"I think we should sit down and talk … "

"I'd like to tell him where he can stick his money."

The door clicked shut behind Adam as he strode into the kitchen, setting a huge bouquet of lilac, white hydrangea, and lavender in a glass vase on the counter. "Whoa, who's sticking money where? That's an awful waste if you ask me, Maddy."

"Worth every penny," Madison mumbled.

"Thank you, sweetie. They're beautiful." Rose touched a flower, breathing in its fresh scent.

"To celebrate this big surprise you and Dad wanted to share tonight," Adam explained.

"Oh, that. You shouldn't have." Rose's voice vibrated as did the hand touching the rose.

Adam raised his eyebrows to Madison in question.

She shrugged her shoulders, giving way to the troublesome thought that her mother's odd behavior and the helicopter in back might be related in some way.

"And what's going on with you, lil' sis? What has your feathers all fluffed up?" He swung an arm around her shoulders.

Madison rolled her eyes. "I'm not explaining the whole thing again. It'll only aggravate me more."

"Give me the shortened version."

"Helicopter landed in the middle of my photo shoot. Arrogant jerk for a pilot. The wedding contract I so desperately needed, gone."

"I didn't know you lost your contract. I'm so sorry." Rose placed a hand over her heart. "I know you'll make it, sweetie. Don't worry."

Adam ruffled Madison's hair. "She's right, you know. Don't sweat it. But if it would make you feel better, I can beat up the jerk pilot for you."

"Arrogant jerk pilot. And yes, it would. Thank you."

He chuckled. "No problem. So not that I won't beat him up for free, but do you think you might be able to help me out tomorrow night at the restaurant? We have a dinner rehearsal and a big anniversary celebration on top of the normal traffic flow."

"Not now," she mumbled under her breath.

She needed the time to revise her business plan and marketing strategy, but Adam had been there for her countless of times and would always be there for her. "Of course, I will."

"Thanks, Maddy." Adam pulled her into a big bear hug, squashing her against his chest. "Now, where's this pilot guy? What does he look like?"

"He's probably still out in the field, fussing over his big boy toy. He's tall, dark hair, blue eyes … "

"Hello, family. There's someone I'd like you to meet." Thomas, her father, came through the door, followed by the very man she was describing. "This is Jake Colt with Colt Enterprises. He's our guest tonight and our surprise. Jake is the new owner of our winery and vineyard."

# CHAPTER TWO

Jake loved a challenge and the golden beauty before him qualified in spades. He watched the color drain from her lovely face even as she pulled herself up to her full height, ready to face whatever he threw at her. She contrasted with the man next to her, whom he assumed was her brother, as his neck flushed red and his hands curled into fists that appeared set to hit him square on in a moment.

"Jake, this is my son, Adam," Thomas said.

Jake put out his hand and kept his voice cordial. It had to be hard to meet the man who now owned your parents' livelihood, but that didn't mean he would back down from a fight, either. "It's a pleasure to meet you."

Adam's face seemed set in stone, but somehow he grabbed Jake's hand—strangling it was more like it—and growled out, "Same."

Jake gripped Adam's hand just as hard and waited for him to release first. The victory went to Jake, but Adam looked ready for round two.

"And this is my daughter, Madison." Thomas motioned to her.

"We've met," Jake said, grinning as she shoved her long, still windswept, blonde hair behind her ears.

"I was afraid of that," Thomas mumbled under his breath.

"Yes, I had the distinct displeasure of running into Mr. Colt in the field." Madison crossed her arms in front of her.

"Madison," Rose rebuked.

Madison grumbled an apology incomprehensible to anyone but herself.

"It's all right, Mrs. Carmichael. Your daughter is allowed to be upset. I believe I interrupted a photo shoot of hers." Jake leaned closer to Madison. "And you can call me Jake. No need to stand on formality."

She shot daggers at him with her eyes. Beautiful, bright blue eyes.

He had gotten under her skin and he wanted to do it again. Women usually swooned around him and men catered to his family's fortune. But the woman before him looked just as ready to punch him in the face as her brother. She intrigued him a great deal. Maybe this lousy assignment his father had sent him on to a slow, backward town wouldn't be without its side perks after all, especially if his father kept up his side of the bargain.

"Jake, why don't we have a drink in my office while dinner is cooking? You haven't tasted a better lasagna than what my Rose makes." Thomas set his hand on his back, steering him out of the room.

"I'll join you," Adam said, moving behind them.

"No," Thomas responded curtly to his son. "Stay here and help your mother."

Jake could see Adam's clenched jaw as he ground his teeth, but he also saw the respect he had for his father as he nodded once and stepped back.

He envied Adam in that moment. He wished he admired his father that much. But he neither respected nor feared Clayton Colt as everyone else did. He merely existed with the corporate mogul who shared his DNA.

After he had finished his drink with Thomas, which was more enjoyable than he thought it would be, they rejoined the rest of the family. The dining room was filled with food and the delicious scents of fresh baked bread and lasagna as they took their seats around a large, oak table. He couldn't remember the last home-cooked meal he'd had, and it smelled better than his favorite five-star restaurants in New York.

Cork curled up on the hardwood floor next to his feet as he scratched the friendly Lab, perhaps his one true ally in the room, behind the ear. Madison scowled at him from across the table, her gaze narrowing on Cork, and he starting rubbing the dog's belly just to irk her some more. She looked like a woman in need of irking.

He bowed his head as the family said grace. The last person in his family who had said grace was his mother when he was a little boy. A needle pricked his heart. This was what small towns did to him, stirred up memories he had pushed away long ago with good reason. And it was exactly why he had to get out of here as fast as he could convince his father.

"So what does it mean that Colt Enterprises bought the winery? For you two, I mean?" Adam asked, throwing his napkin down in front of him, his food forgotten.

"The winery hasn't been making it for some time now," Thomas said. "Your mother and I have tried to keep it afloat but the last few years have been rough. More and more large scale wineries are popping up in the surrounding areas with resources that far surpass ours and prices we can't touch. Tourists are flocking to them and beginning to bypass Serenity Creek's boutique wineries all together. Clayton Colt, Jake's father, approached us with a deal we couldn't overlook."

"What exactly are the details of this great deal?" Madison pursued with a tilt to her stubbornly set jaw.

Jake didn't miss the quick glance she stole in his direction. Nor did he miss the spark of attraction in her eyes buried under all her carefully controlled emotions.

So she wasn't entirely immune to his charms.

"Well, Colt Enterprises now owns the winery in full, but they've agreed to keep me on as head winemaker and your mom as the general manager," Thomas answered.

"What about the house?" Madison asked.

Rose spoke up, her voice calm and quiet. "The house is separate from the winery, as is the land it's built upon. We've retained ownership of the house, but not the winery or the vineyards."

Adam thumped his hand onto the table, causing a clattering of dishes around them. "You never said you were in financial trouble. I could have helped you."

Thomas sighed. "I appreciate that, son, but you don't have that kind of money."

"I would have found a way. I would have … "

Madison settled her hand on Adam's arm and shook her head, no doubt a silent warning not to go down that path. She turned to Jake and it obviously took all her strength to keep herself from tearing him apart with her bare hands as the look she sent him clearly said she wanted to do.

"So, Jake, what plans do you have for Oak Hills? How are you going to turn things around?" she asked, her eyebrow arched in challenge.

In truth, he didn't have any ideas for the winery, nor did he care anything about it. He didn't even want to be here and wouldn't be if his father hadn't dangled business freedom in front of him. All he had to do was turn the winery around to make a decent profit, and Clayton would give him complete rein over whatever acquisition division he wanted to head up in the company in the States or overseas.

He knew it was a power play on Clayton's part. He expected this job to convince Jake how much he needed to learn from his father, including his dirty tricks, to carry on under him. There was no other reason his father could possibly be interested in such a small property when Colt Enterprises dealt in big time real estate. It was a low risk investment on his part to get what he wanted from Jake.

Still, Jake couldn't imagine abandoning the company entirely. As calculating as Clayton was, he and Colt Enterprises were all he had. But putting as much geographical space between him and his father sounded good, real good.

"I have a few thoughts on how to turn a profit with the winery." He smirked and couldn't help having a little fun. "Maybe we should expand it into a big time destination winery complete with a resort and spa."

Madison's mouth dropped open and a vein throbbed in Adam's neck.

"You can't turn my family's lovely, boutique winery into some tourist monstrosity. What is wrong with you? This is what you get when you have some big city dweller who doesn't know a thing about wine come into our town and take over. You, you … " Madison stammered, searching for her next word.

This time Adam squeezed her shoulder. They had the sibling non-verbal cues down, he'd give them that.

Did she always have such a wild temper? Or was it just he who ruffled her constructed façade of composure? He hoped so.

He put his hands up in a cease-fire. "I'm joking. I would never do something so extreme. Unless the situation called for it."

Although, expanding the winery somewhat might be a necessity to pull in the kind of traffic needed to turn the business around and get him out of this speck of dust.

Thomas and Rose laughed uneasily, apparently trying to break the tight tension in the room crackling from their children.

"No, you're just extreme enough to land a helicopter in someone's field like you own the place," Madison bristled.

He stared at her in silence.

He thought it best not to point out that he did in fact own the property, but she must have realized that truth on her own as her cheeks burned red.

Jake leaned forward. "Perhaps I can take you flying sometime. It might help with this aversion you seem to have to my MD 600N."

"Your what?"

"My helicopter."

"I don't fly."

"You don't fly?"

"I don't fly," she repeated with more force.

They locked eyes with each other, engaged in a visual battle. He heard the uneasy fidgeting coming from Rose in the seat next to him.

"Let's move into the living room for dessert," she said, rising from her chair on shaky legs.

Jake never stopped looking at Madison. "I can't imagine what amazing concoction you have for dessert, Mrs. Carmichael. I've never tasted better food."

"Please call me Rose and don't mind my daughter's rudeness."

At that, Madison fell back in her chair, breaking eye contact to watch her mother's exit before shifting her glance to the still full plate of food before her.

Jake enjoyed the sweet taste of victory. His stay here might actually be bearable if he could spend it with this spitfire.

• • •

"I don't understand why you didn't tell us the winery was in such despair. Adam and I would have done everything we could to help you out." Madison dried a dinner plate before putting it away in the cupboard.

She knew her brother was having the same conversation with their father in his office now that Jake, the way too good-looking intruder, had left.

"I know, and your father and I love you both for it. But neither of you has the kind of resources it's going to take to turn things around and we know neither of you is interested in running the winery." Rose patted Madison's arm before finishing up with organizing the leftovers in the refrigerator.

Guilt burned Madison's gut. Their parents hadn't pushed Adam or her; they taught their children to go after their dreams no matter what, but she knew it hurt them, especially her father, that she didn't want a piece of what they had built from the ground up.

And now look at what had happened to their aspirations. What if she had taken over the winery, as her dad had wanted? Would she have been able to save them from having to sell? Would she have been able to help them keep what they had developed? Maybe. It certainly would have taken some of the burden off of them.

"I'm sorry, Mom. I should have been here."

Rose stopped putting away containers and grabbed Madison's shoulders. "Sweetie, there is nothing you could have done. Your father and I are okay with this sale. It's not ideal, but we get to continue working the vineyard and we have the house. More importantly, we have each other."

Madison stared down at her feet.

Rose tilted up her head to look her in the eye. "Family is more essential than any business."

But the winery wasn't any business. It was their dream. Their blood, sweat, and tears.

She hugged her mom tight. "I love you."

"I love you too, sweetie." Rose pulled back and touched Madison's wavy hair. "You could help us out by being a little nicer to the owner's son. He is here to oversee the winery."

She cringed. "I know. I'm sorry. It was the shock of everything." At least she hoped that explained why she seemed to continually lose her self-control around the man.

The idea of being polite to him, though, inflamed every nerve in her being. He was the enemy.

Cork sidled up to her legs.

She cast him a long glance, whispering, "Don't think I've forgiven you, yet. I saw you at dinner."

She patted his head all the same.

"He's a handsome one. Very charming," Rose said, a hint of mischief in her tone.

Madison rolled her eyes. "And doesn't he know it."

Only her mother would look past all the guy's haughty smugness to his few good traits. Tucker had the same arrogance about him and look how well that had turned out for her. What was it with city dwellers that made them think they were better than everyone else?

"Well, I'm sure he's used to being catered to. He's rich, good looking, and a nice boy."

Madison didn't know about the "nice boy" part. She could be pleasant to the guy, or at least try, but cater to him? Never.

She finished wiping down the counter and glanced out the window above the sink at the neatly lined rows of grape vines laden with fruit. She'd be devastated if someone stole her photography business—her baby, her life's work—from her after all she had put into it.

No way could she stand by and let this happen to her family. She was going to do everything in her power to salvage their dream. She would get the winery back for them in any way she could, and she'd start by getting rid of Jake Colt.

•••

Jake nursed a glass of the Grand Marnier he had found in the well-stocked mini fridge of his suite while pouring over the dossier on the Oak Hills winery and the family behind it. When he'd first been given the packet, he hadn't given it a second look. How hard could turning a profit at some trivial winery be? But after meeting the Carmichaels' daughter, maybe he should give the information more attention.

A picture of Madison smiled up at him from the simple, dark wood desk that matched the rest of the bed and breakfast style furniture in the room. He knew it had been taken from her website, as he'd already perused that as well. The folder, though, provided more in-depth background on her and all of the family members. His father paid to be well informed, and this was no exception.

Madison's photography skills were good from what her website showed. But her business was floundering and her attempts to switch over to wedding photography were also failing. Her latest effort had been to photograph the upcoming wedding of some movie producer's daughter by the name of Victoria Temple. That must have been the photo shoot he had disrupted.

She should have taken the money he had offered her. She needed it desperately, and he had been more than generous considering he had landed on his own property. Well, his father's property. Why hadn't she taken it?

That was the problem with dealing with rural business owners. Too much pride and not enough common sense. He hated small towns, everything about them, which wasn't saying much since nothing happened in them except the incessant gossip about people's affairs that was really nobody's business in the first place.

He listened for the smallest sound and, even in the inn, couldn't hear anything but the rustle of some tree branches outside. When did you ever hear trees rustling in a city unless a plane was coming in for a landing over them?

He could smell the freshly baked oatmeal cookie the maid set on the nightstand earlier. It promised to taste as sweet as the apple pie Rose Carmichael had made for dessert. All signs of a small town, and each one a rope trying to lasso the memories he kept smothered under fast cars, beautiful women, and one thrill-seeking adventure after another.

His phone buzzed and his father's name appeared on the screen.

"Clayton," Jake growled.

"Hello, Jake. How was dinner?" His father's deep, commanding voice reverberated through the phone.

"Everything was home-cooked and made from scratch."

"I meant about the business. You're supposed to be there to work, not play." Clayton's words carried a sharp bite to them.

Jake's were no different. "Business went slow like everything else in this backward town you banished me to."

"Time for you to grow up, Jake. I can't run this corporation forever, and you need to be ready to take over my legacy."

That sounded fine, but with his father it really meant towing the line and being another one of his puppets, all strings attached all the time. "Cut the sob story. This isn't about the corporation, it never has been. It's always been about control. And this assignment doesn't matter one bit to your company. At the end of this, I expect you to honor your end of our little arrangement."

Clayton chuckled. "Two sides to every coin, but it's still the same coin and my side is right. The sooner you realize that, the better. How's the inn working out?"

Jake clenched his fingers, choking the glass he still held. He threw back the amber-colored liquid. "Great, considering you own a perfectly good estate a mere thirty minutes away that I could be staying at right now instead."

Clayton gave a low, grating chuckle. "Too much distraction. You need to focus on the winery and how you're going to turn a profit there with our investment."

Well, at least Madison had turned out to be one of the more beautiful distractions he'd ever seen. He could definitely see turning a profit with that investment.

"Jake, the sooner you bring that winery around, the sooner you can come home."

What home?

"So long as I get to do this my way." Jake already had fragments of a plan.

"So long as your way is in line with mine. I'm serious. This is your last chance." The steel in Clayton's voice would make any sane man tremble and displayed all the command he was known for in the business world.

Only Jake knew that coldness extended far beyond business—it went right down to Clayton's very soul. Jake was no fool, but he also never backed down from a challenge.

"Don't make threats you can't carry out, especially when I couldn't care less about them." Except he did want to get out of this town and fast. He detested obeying his father in coming here but it was still better than being in the corporate office with him in person. Flying around Europe or China—that's where he wanted to be and where he would go just as soon as he got out of here. "I already have a plan to turn things around."

"That's good, Jake. Real good, because you're on thin ice and it's getting thinner."

Jake beamed, holding up the picture of Madison. What better way to mix a little business with a lot of pleasure? If his father only knew what his plan entailed, he would say the ice had already broken.

# CHAPTER THREE

"They sold the winery."

The words still sounded foreign to Madison.

"What?" Tessa shrieked.

Madison sat across from her best friend at a wrought iron patio table in the corner of Serenity Creek's quaint coffeehouse and bakery, the only one in town. Positioned on Oak Street, the city's main drag lined with dozens of oak trees, it offered a wide view of everyone's comings and goings, but right now her focus rested on filling her need for caffeine and solving the looming problem before her.

She cradled her steaming mug with the word "Lily's" scribbled on the side close to her, savoring the rich aroma of the dark roast coffee.

Madison massaged her temple with her free hand. "To some big shot real estate tycoon no less. I'm still shocked. Colt Enterprises now owns Oak Hills."

Tessa Gianini whistled, tossing her chestnut brown hair over her shoulder. "They're huge. I've come across their name in quite a few business articles in the past. Oak Hills is a tiny property compared to what they normally buy. I'm surprised they were interested."

"It's my fault. If I hadn't been so preoccupied with getting my photography going, I could have helped my parents."

"That's nonsense. And this isn't the end of the world. Has Colt Enterprises sent a representative yet?"

The fact that some conceited city dweller now called the shots at her parents' boutique winery did make it the end of the world. Her world at least.

Madison laughed, a sarcastic crack in the peaceful morning air. "Oh yeah, they did. Jake Colt. The man is insufferable."

"So he's hot?"

Madison smiled at how well her friend knew her. "Very much so, and so off limits it's not even funny. Not that it matters, though. I concluded that high-powered executives aren't my type after Tucker."

Tessa shrugged. "What do you expect? The guy is the only son of a multi-millionaire. He lives in a completely different world than we do."

Boy, wasn't that the truth? He flew helicopters; she drove a beat up, barely still alive car. She glanced at the aging Toyota parked on the street with its faded blue paint. At least it had started today after only two attempts.

"Why did Colt Enterprises send the owner's son, though?" Tessa said. "I think he's a VP or something there. Why would they send someone so high profile for such a small operation?"

Madison shook her head. "I don't know. I don't care. I just want him gone."

"Sounds like you have a plan."

"Not yet, but I'm working on it. Speaking of plans, I have good news and I have bad news. The bad news is that I lost the Addison-Temple wedding. The good news is that now I have more time to spend on those ad shots you wanted."

Tessa sucked in a breath. "I'm so sorry. I know what that client meant to you. There'll be others, though."

"Eventually, yeah. But at the moment, I have a more pressing problem looming before me." Madison took a large drink of her coffee, relishing the warm sunlight bathing the tiny coffeehouse. With the muffled sound of bells wafting from the spire of city hall in Serenity Square, the early morning could have been perfect and peaceful if not for the stubborn, but oh so steamy, predicament that had barged into her life yesterday.

She saw the teasing glint in Tessa's eyes and didn't appreciate it one bit.

"I know that look. No, he's not a dating option. No way, not in a million years. Even if he weren't my sworn enemy, we're too different. I could never live in his rich, fast-paced world, and I wouldn't want to."

"I'll admit you two are at opposite ends of the spectrum, but you never know."

Madison shook her head. "I'm not going anywhere near a big city or its inhabitants unless absolutely necessary. One mugging and betrayal is good enough for me. You're in danger of becoming just like your mother. Matchmaker extraordinaire for the people who don't want to be matched up."

Tessa sputtered over her latte. "Excuse me? Take it back. Right now."

Madison put up her hands in surrender. "Okay, okay, I take it back."

"You know she already heard the gossip about a new hunk in town. She's determined to marry me or one of my sisters off to him."

"You guys are welcome to him."

"No, thanks. The simple fact that Mom is pushing him means he's a no. And the way you're fretting over him tells me you're more interested than you'd like." Tessa lowered her lashes, hiding behind her mug. "She then moved on to how he would be perfect for you. Especially since you've already met him and he landed in your vineyard and all."

"Excuse me?" Madison's shoulders tensed with indignant apprehension. As if she wasn't capable of finding a good, long lasting relationship on her own. After a few tragic dating attempts, including one Tucker White, Madison had given Ava Gianini the firm, yet kind request to stay away from her love life. A request

Ava appeared determined to ignore. Still, an ache lodged in her heart. She couldn't help but feel the lack of romance in her life.

She rolled her shoulders and took a fortifying sip of coffee. Her photography came first, and she didn't have time for such distractions as men and romance.

She pulled out a folder labeled with Tessa's name from her leather satchel, a cherished gift from her brother. "These are copies of some of the photos we took at last year's harvest festival for your ads. Look them over and let me know what you want to tweak, add, or forget about for this year."

Tessa accepted the file. "I really wish you would let me pay you for all of your hard work. Especially with the Addison-Temple wedding falling through."

"Not a chance. You're my best friend. You've been there for me through everything since we were in diapers. I'm not taking a penny from you."

"You can be so stubborn sometimes." Tessa sighed.

"I know. It's one of my better traits."

"Not really."

Madison smiled. "Agree to disagree."

"You'll make a fine opponent for the mysterious Jake Colt. Where are you going to start?"

"Well, you know what they say. Keep your friends close and your enemies closer."

• • •

Madison powered down her laptop for the day and started packing it up along with the external hard drive with the pictures she planned to edit tonight over a microwave dinner. She had just zipped up her bag when the bells on her office door jingled. Now what?

She stood up but couldn't see more than a shadow as the blinding setting sun poured in through the large front windows facing the small side street outside.

Squinting, she finally saw the broad shoulders, muscled chest, and dark, rustled hair of a familiar figure. His presence filled the small room. Her stomach dropped, but she refused to let him see any of her turmoil.

"Hello, Madison." Jake moved to stand on the other side of her desk.

"Mr. Colt. What can I do for you?" Her words rang out clipped and direct.

"I told you to call me Jake."

"I'd rather not. We're not that familiar."

"Mr. Colt is my father, and I won't answer to the same name as him." His eyes froze like blue ice chips.

She nodded, surprised at his acute need to separate from his dad. "All right, fair enough. How did you find me?"

One side of his mouth quirked up. "This place isn't that big. I asked around."

Lovely. Now the whole town would be talking about this stranger and wondering his connection to her.

She kept her satchel in front of her on the table as a barrier between them, but she couldn't block the delectable sight of him or the fresh scent of soap he carried. She gulped. "How can I help you?"

"You can have dinner with me."

Her pulse accelerated. "Excuse me?"

"I'd like to take you to dinner tonight. I want to talk about a proposal I have for Oak Hills."

"Shouldn't you be discussing that with my dad?"

"It involves you so I thought it best we go over it together first."

She tensed. "If you're trying to gain me as an ally in some sort of scheme against my dad's wishes, you couldn't have chosen a worse person."

He rocked back on his heels. "Relax. I know you better than you think. You have a pretty low opinion of me if you believe I would do something so callous."

"You don't know anything about me."

He set his hands on her desk, bending toward her until his face stopped mere inches from her. "But I'd like to."

She dug her fingers into her bag. She knew she needed to say something but words escaped her.

He continued on in a low, husky voice. "We're going to be seeing a lot of each other. It is a small town. I think you should at least hear what I have to say. Who knows, you might actually like my plan."

She tilted her head to the side, hands on her hips, desperate to regain her cool before he saw what his close proximity did to her. Why not spend some time with him? Wasn't her intention all along to keep an eye on him? What better way to read her opponent in order to devise a plan to get rid of him and help her parents at the same time? "All right, fine. Dinner. Just let me close up."

He moved back to the door and she breathed a sigh of relief.

Straightening her posture, she grabbed her handbag. Her family's winery was too important for her to ruin everything with her insane attraction to some wealthy city guy. She needed to keep her head on straight and remember what she was doing here.

Madison followed Jake's lead as they strolled through the quaint downtown area before stopping in front of The Wine Cork.

She glanced up at his profile. He had to know the restaurant belonged to her brother. "You're brave."

He grinned.

Oh yeah, he knew.

"This restaurant came highly recommended, and I thought it would be good to support your family now that we're partners and all."

The spark in his eyes told a different story. He was here to provoke Adam.

She folded her arms. "I hope you know what you're getting yourself into. Adam's not as forgiving as I am."

He held open the door for her. "You've forgiven me? That's good to know."

She stomped past him into the restaurant. "Not even a little bit."

He walked in behind her, rubbing his chest. "Ouch, that hurts."

She shook her head but couldn't help smiling.

Rich scents of steak, sauces, and wine washed over her from the bustling dining room. Couples filled the wooden bar, laughing with drinks in hand. She adjusted to the dim lighting from the overhead chandeliers in time to see her brother.

Adam stormed up behind the maitre d' like a lion ready to pounce.

"What are you doing here?" He locked eyes with Jake, before taking in Madison. "And why are you here with him?"

She shook her head. "I didn't pick this place."

Adam cocked his head to the side and raised his eyebrows, letting her know she hadn't fooled him. She was avoiding his actual question of what she was doing out and about with Jake.

Jake's voice was steady, yet unyielding beside her. "Relax. I brought her here to discuss business. This isn't a date or anything."

Adam bristled, and from the wary look on his face, she thought he might refuse to serve Jake.

Not that she blamed him. She might actually enjoy the scene. Mr. High and Mighty thrown out on his rear.

"This way," Adam said, his words gruff as he led the way to a table in the middle of the busy room where he no doubt could see them from anywhere in the restaurant.

Adam reached to pull out her chair, but Jake beat him to it. The two stood inches apart, staring at each other like bulls ready to charge. All of the noises of chatter, clanging dishes, and a cacophony of other sounds faded into the vortex of the tension between the two men.

She slipped into the chair and out of the danger zone.

Jake came around the table and took his own seat, never letting Adam out of his line of sight.

Adam leaned down next to her. "If he so much as looks at you the wrong way, give me the signal and I'll throw him out."

"Thanks. I'll be fine," she whispered.

Adam gave Jake one last warning glare before walking over to the bar and a patron who had signaled for his attention.

Jake picked up his menu. "I'm glad that's out of the way. Is he like that with every guy you go out with?"

Her heart fluttered. "I'm not going out with you. You said so yourself, this isn't a date."

"So Adam's easier on your dates than on your business partners?"

She smirked. If Jake had been her date, Adam never would have seated them. "My brother's very protective of his loved ones."

"Something you two share in common."

She stilled her hand on the menu. How had he picked up on that? She didn't see him as the type of guy to notice anything beyond his own sphere of influence, let alone a small nuance of her personality.

"You should try the rib eye. It's amazing," she said, anything to break the spell.

"Good evening. Madison, always a pleasure to see you," Greg, their waiter, greeted them.

"Thanks, Greg. How's your family?" she asked.

"They're doing great. Leslie is starting kindergarten this year. What can I get you two to start with?"

Before she could respond, Jake spoke up.

"We'll have a bottle of the Villa Toscana and an order of your baked Brie and flatbread."

Greg dipped his head. "Very good. I'll be right back with your wine."

She sat back in her chair. A guy had never ordered for her before; she had never let them. "Should I give Greg my menu now or do I get to choose my own meal?"

"I'm sorry. Do you not like baked Brie?"

It was her favorite, but she would withstand torture before she admitted that to him. Especially after the guy had the nerve to order something other than an Oak Hills wine when he was the new owner and the business was struggling.

At her silence, he continued. "I happen to love baked Brie and my source told me this place has the best in town. Besides the fact that there is only one other place in town that serves it."

"Your source being, who? Eddie, the concierge at the Maple Grove Inn?"

The surprise on his face lit her up inside. One point for her.

"Do you know everyone in town?"

"I've lived here my whole life."

"So, yes you do. And how did you know where I'm staying?"

She shrugged. "It's a small town. Word travels fast."

She saw the shadow cross his face.

"That is does," he grumbled, picking up his menu and pointing to the cover. "Was the dog named after the restaurant?"

She grinned at his sarcastic note. He was making a joke, but little did he know he wasn't far off the mark. "Actually, the restaurant's named after the dog."

His eyebrows drew together. "Excuse me."

"Cork is Adam's dog. A Christmas gift while we were in high school. At the time, Adam imagined he would follow in Dad's footsteps with the winery and was pretty entrenched in learning the ropes. It was then he discovered a winery really wasn't where he wanted to be."

"He didn't stray too far."

"No, but far enough for him. When he opened the restaurant, he picked the name as a play on words. Being a town centered on vineyards, The Wine Cork fit right in, but really he named it after the dog. He loves that no one gets the connection."

"I did."

"You got lucky," she shot back.

He chuckled. "If your brother got a puppy for Christmas that year, what did you get? A pony?"

"My first real camera. Sealed my fate as a photographer."

She opened her mouth to launch into another story, but caught herself. What was she doing opening up to this interloper? And why was it such an easy thing to do?

Their waiter appeared at the perfect moment, albeit later than Madison would have preferred. He could have shown up before she started dishing out family stories.

"Here we go. The Villa Toscana. An excellent choice, sir," Greg announced, presenting the bottle for Jake's appraisal.

At Jake's nod, Greg opened the wine and poured a small sampling for him. Once Jake tasted it and signaled for him to proceed, the waiter filled both wine glasses and set the bottle on the table between them, alongside the candle and single red rose bud.

"Are you ready to order?" he asked.

They put in their orders and Greg left them to relay their selections to the kitchen.

She swirled her glass. She never really drank foreign wines. She swallowed the deep red liquid and discovered Jake had a very good sense of vintages. The wine was amazing, but their vineyard's was better. And less than half the price.

"What do you think?" he asked.

"It's good," she answered, reluctantly.

He bowed his head. "I'm glad you enjoy it. I tasted this wine in Italy when it was first released."

Of course he had. He probably flew there in a private jet, no less.

"Have you ever been to Tuscany?" he asked.

"No. I meant what I said last night. I don't fly."

He set his glass down, shock apparent on his face. "Never? Have you ever even been on a plane?"

"We don't need to get into it."

"Okay. So, where have you traveled to?"

She squirmed. "Nowhere. I've never been outside of California."

He folded his arms on the table. "You're not really the adventurous type, are you?"

"Not all of us can be as carefree to land helicopters in fields whenever they like and take off to Italy when they're in the mood."

He chuckled. "That should make this all the more interesting."

"What are you talking about?"

Greg returned with their appetizer and she waited with bated breath until he left them alone again.

Jake made no move to explain. Instead, he cut into the warm baked Brie and slid some onto her plate along with a piece of grilled flatbread before taking a slice for himself.

"What are you up to?" she blurted out.

"Are you sure you don't want to eat before you hear my proposal?"

She twisted her napkin tightly in her hand. What game was he playing?

"You think you're so charming, don't you?"

"Some say I am."

"Well, I don't. You said we were going to talk business, so let's talk. What are you planning?"

He set his fork aside, dabbing the corners of his mouth with his napkin. "You're right. We are here to discuss business."

Remorse sank in. He might be her enemy, but she had promised her parents she would try to be polite and here she was not even letting him enjoy the food he had ordered. Why did he put her so on edge?

"I'm sorry, I'm being rude. Let's take a step back and talk rationally while we eat this delicious appetizer. Eddie's right, it is the best. And I'm not saying that because this is my brother's restaurant."

He winked. "Now, we're talking, sweetness."

Did he just say "sweetness"? Unease, suspicion, and delight rolled through her all at once.

"So, what do you think of Oak Hills?" she asked, digging into the food in front of her.

"It's a small winery with fairly good wine and its own old-fashioned appeal, but no one knows about it. Which is why I'm considering a marketing blitz to increase awareness."

She dropped her fork onto her plate with a clang.

He put his hands up. "Easy, easy. I know you don't want an army of tourists invading your precious town, but you do need some traffic in here. That's part of Oak Hills's current problem, remember? No customers, no money."

She grudgingly picked up her fork again. "You do have a point."

"Sorry, what was that? Did you actually concede something to me?"

"Don't push your luck, Colt."

He grinned. "Always."

She softened her shoulders. "Tell me more about this marketing idea of yours."

"We highlight what this area is all about. We work with local businesses to offer cross promotions. A discount at such and such establishment with the purchase of two bottles of Oak Hills wine and so forth."

The idea had merit. The local business owners wouldn't necessarily like working with an outsider, but they wouldn't consider such a broad reaching promotion from anyone with less influence and money than Jake.

She leaned in. "Where do I come in? You said this plan of yours involved me."

He inched closer to her across the table. "It does. I need you to take the pictures we'll use to advertise the cross promotions. You'll be well compensated, of course."

She blinked rapidly, a thousand thoughts spinning in her head.

"Here we are. A medium rare rib eye and the pasta primavera for you, Madison."

Greg set their plates in front of them and cleared his throat. "Is there anything else I can get you?"

Jake waited for her response.

She kept silent, uncertain what to say next.

Greg raised his eyebrows. "If you need something, let me know."

He walked away and Madison still tried to make sense of Jake's proposition.

Could this be a pity offer to make up for the money he cost her by ruining her shoot the other day? He could afford to bring up a big shot photographer from Los Angeles. He didn't need her. She refused to take a handout, especially from him.

But what if his proposal was genuine? She had no doubt the marketing would help the winery. The sooner it turned a profit, the sooner she could get rid of Jake and turn him into a remote owner until she and Adam could pull together the finances to buy back the winery.

Not to mention, the job would give her the greatest exposure she had ever had, and, realistically, her business couldn't survive without some kind of cash infusion, and fast. He owed her and it was a job. She would work for the money and it would be the best work she had ever done.

She wouldn't get a better chance to help her parents, solidify her photography business, and force Jake out of town all in one swoop.

Jake must have seen the war raging within her.

"Come on, don't you want to help your parents?"

Yes. And she wanted him out of her life. But she knew better than to trust him, so she had to proceed with caution.

"What's the catch?"

He shook his head. "No catch. It's a basic business strategy. You're a good photographer, and I thought you would want to assist your family." A teasing glint lit his face. "I have personal experience of how protective you are of them."

She laughed and the knots in her neck began to loosen. "So you tell me what you want shot around town and I take those pictures?"

"Something like that."

She narrowed her eyes. "Describe that something."

"We might need to expand our horizons a little outside of the immediate vicinity, not too far, but I want to include the beach area as well. And we'll go together to the locations. I have specific ideas in mind, and I like to take a hands-on approach."

The sweltering look in his eyes told her what kind of hands-on approach he was accustomed to, and she was certain it always involved women.

Apprehension seeped through her blood. Close contact with him spelled all kinds of trouble. His handsome face and physique were not lost on her, but she knew better than to give in to his charms. Underneath that gorgeous exterior lay a rich, spoiled man used to having everything handed to him. She could resist him.

She stared straight at him and saw the goading look in his eyes. He was daring her, and she refused to back down.

"As long as your hands stay on work and nothing else, then we have a deal." She reached her arm out over the table.

"You might want to change your terms later on, but for right now, we have a deal."

He grabbed her hand and a hot current shot from his fingers up her arm and straight through her.

"Everything going okay over here?" Adam asked, taking in their handshake.

Madison pulled away abruptly.

"Everything's great. Madison has just agreed to help with a marketing plan I have for your parents' winery." Jake smiled at her before staring up at Adam. "Great food, by the way."

Adam clenched his jaw. "I'm glad it meets with your superior approval. Maddy, can I have a word with you, please?"

Adam's hand grasped her elbow and all but yanked her out of the chair.

"Of course. I'll be right back," she said to Jake.

Adam tugged her to a corner of the room, outside the doors leading to the kitchen.

"Are you out of your mind?" he hissed.

Resentment swelled within her. "Not at all. Do you have a better idea to help Mom and Dad?"

Adam opened his mouth to speak but shut it again.

"That's what I thought. I can keep an eye on this guy, get him out of Dad's way, and help get the winery the customers it needs."

Adam shook his head. "I don't want you working with him. I don't trust him and I don't like the way he looks at you."

She ignored the excitement his words triggered in her.

"Neither do I. Don't worry."

"You're my sister. I always worry about you."

She hugged him. "Too much. You never back off."

"That's because you land yourself in trouble all the time."

She pulled herself up to her full height. "I do not, and I am perfectly capable of taking care of myself."

"I know, Maddy. But not this time. Not with him. You're playing with fire."

She forced all of her courage into her words. "I know what I'm doing."

Inside she was less certain, but she wouldn't let Adam or anyone else see her insecurity.

She turned to walk back to their table. Jake sat there, relaxing back in his chair, appearing every bit the striking playboy. The sexy look he sent her across the room seared her skin and clenched her gut. What had she just signed herself up for?

# CHAPTER FOUR

Clayton's dooming ringtone blared through his sleep. Jake opened his groggy eyes to a still dark room and a clock that said five in the morning in big, glaring red digits. He sat up in bed, annoyed, peeved, and fumbling for his cell phone.

"Did you even think of the time difference and the fact that you're three hours ahead?" Jake bit out.

"Of course I did, right before I called you. Nothing wrong with getting up at 5:00 a.m. You should do it more often."

The uncharacteristic cheerfulness in Clayton's voice at waking him up exasperated Jake's last nerve.

"Tell me what you want and make it fast."

Clayton's words became like hard, cold stone. "You should be working on the Oak Hills job, not sleeping the day away. At five, I was in the company gym. At six, I was at my desk. You're still in bed. I sent you our plan for the property; you just have to implement it. Have you even read it?"

He'd read it, many times. It was the same strategy Clayton used for all of the properties he bought. Tear it down and build it better. But he refused to do things under Clayton's management. If he was stuck in this small, nowhere town with the smallest property in their portfolio, he would handle it on his own terms.

"I've read it and I'm not doing it."

"What?" Clayton exclaimed, his fury vibrated through the phone.

Jake didn't flinch. "You heard me. Remember, we're doing this my way. I already have a marketing strategy I'm putting into place." He smiled, thinking of Madison's lush, blonde hair and smooth curves.

Clayton huffed. "Difficult. You've always been so difficult."

As if his father had ever taken the time to know him.

"Send me your idea and I'll look it over," he commanded.

"I don't think so."

"Excuse me? Do you think I'm just going to give you free rein to do as you please with my company?"

"Yes, because that's what this is all about, isn't it? You trying to get me more involved in the company, and under your puppet strings. I could completely blow this project and it wouldn't even register on the company's financial radar. You want to play this out? These are the new rules. We try my idea first."

Clayton's strategy would have him here for ages overseeing the process. His plan could get him to the Alps, and far away from his father's clutches, in a quarter of that time or less. Not to mention the primary benefit of spending time with Madison, his true motivation for putting together such a business scheme. Plus, he would satiate his need for thrills, as much as that was possible in this backward piece of real estate. And if he ever needed an escape from his pesky childhood memories, it was now when they were being thrown in his face.

"All right," Clayton finally said. "But don't think you can get away with this moving forward. You get your chance to prove yourself, and then I expect you to take your place under me. Someone has to carry on my legacy."

"And I'm all you've got," Jake said what he knew Clayton was thinking. "Great chat, Clayton. Let's do it again sometime when the sun's up."

He hung up and tossed his phone on the nightstand, punching the pillow a few times before lying back down in bed. Jake had just gotten comfortable again when his cell phone rang for the second time. He snatched up the phone without even shifting the covers.

Madison's name popped up on the screen.

He grinned as he answered. "Good morning, sunshine."

"I'm sorry, did I wake you?"

The teasing tinge to her voice told him that had been her devious plan all along.

He grinned. "Actually, I was already up."

"Oh." She gave a disappointed sigh.

He sat up to lean against the headboard. "What can I do for you?"

"I thought we should meet this morning to discuss what pictures you want taken for the winery."

"Sounds good. Why don't I treat you to breakfast? Your choice this time."

"No," she said in a rush. "I mean, I'll cover breakfast. I don't need you to buy me everything. This is a business relationship, not a personal one. How about some coffee and pastries at Lily's?"

He chuckled. A woman had never offered to buy him anything in his life. Not just a pretty face after all. He respected her need to stand her ground.

"What's so funny? You're my client and I take clients out from time to time."

Knowing the state of her finances, he highly doubted she did so often.

He stopped laughing. "I apologize. I'll agree to you getting breakfast if you bring it to the airport and meet me there."

"Not a chance, Colt."

"I'd love to take you up flying. I can't believe you've never been on a plane."

"Believe it and get over it."

What did she have against flying? Was it a fear of hers? Time for a new tactic.

"All right, then. Bring breakfast to go and meet me in the lobby. Dress casually."

He went through a mental list of the preparations he would need to make.

"Why?"

"You'll be more comfortable."

"For what?"

"Just trust me."

"Yeah, right."

He ran a hand through his hair. She was a tough one.

"Madison, you can meet me with breakfast and sneakers on, or I can pick you up for breakfast by the beach in Santa Barbara. Your choice."

The line went silent for a few seconds before Madison answered, her words clipped. "Fine. I'll see you in an hour at your hotel."

"Great. See you then."

He set his phone down, stretched, and then walked to the bathroom for a hot shower.

Amazing how he didn't even need coffee to get out of bed so early. Sparring with Madison energized him more than caffeine.

Based on his research on the area, he knew the perfect spot to take her. He couldn't wait to get back outdoors. He had been stuck inside for far too long.

He called the concierge to procure another backpack, large water bottle, and some boots in various women's sizes, figuring one of them had to fit Madison, then got a hold of Tasty Treats, a boutique caterer in town the concierge recommended, to arrange a picnic lunch complete with a bottle of Oak Hills wine. He made sure to mention his cross promotion idea with the Carmichaels' winery to them. Now, he could be truthful, if not entirely honest, when he told Madison their outing had to do with business.

He stepped into the scalding water, leaning against the tiles and letting the spray run down his face and body. He'd never been so challenged by a woman. Women flocked to him, but not Madison. She fought him where others caved, she resisted where others accepted. And he figured somewhere in there, a passion called out to him to be set free. It's what made her irresistible. It was time to loosen up Madison's tightly wound restraint.

• • •

Madison paced the lobby, clutching two cups of coffee and a bag of chocolate croissants from Lily's. She had arrived early, uncertain and more than a little hesitant for whatever secret arrangements Jake intended for the day.

She came to an abrupt halt the moment she spotted him, right on time, strolling down the staircase, confident and sure of himself. He wore jeans and a shirt as well as he did the slacks and polo shirt he had donned last night. With his dark hair slicked back, still wet from a shower, and his sapphire-blue eyes zeroing in on her, he looked every bit the ruggedly handsome man talked about all over town. She noticed he carried two backpacks. Neither appeared to be a good sign of what awaited her.

"Coffee and breakfast as promised." She held out a cup to him and shook the bag in her hand.

Jake traded one backpack for the cup. "Thank you."

She held the backpack at arm's length. "What is in here and why do I need it?"

"It's a surprise." He took a long sip of coffee.

"I don't like surprises."

"I know. It's something I'm hoping to change."

How did she respond to such a statement?

He hitched his backpack over his shoulder, already walking to the door. "Come on, we can eat on the way."

She sighed, having no choice but to follow him and whatever crazy events he had arranged.

She settled in next to him in his rented Range Rover. Of course, he would drive such a car. She ran her hand along the buttery smooth, gray leather seat. A far cry from the battered, brown upholstery in her own car.

He drove them out to the main highway while nibbling on one of the delectable croissants.

She grabbed a piece of her own and glanced over her shoulder at the backseat where a picnic basket rested on the floor.

"What's that?" she asked, pointing to the container.

He dismissed her question with a wave of his hand. "That's for later."

No way could he be this irritating by accident. "Are you seriously not going to tell me anything about where you're taking me and what we're doing?"

"Yes."

His simple answer annoyed her more than a long explanation of his reasoning.

She hated not being in control. How had she lost it so fast? She had to gain direction of the situation again and get things moving toward where she wanted them.

"Are buying wineries and aggravating women your main goals in life or do you have other interests?"

He chuckled. "Believe it or not, I've never worked with a winery before and most women find me anything but aggravating. Or so I've been told."

"They've lied."

He glanced over at her. "Really?"

No. She knew perfectly well what most women must say about him. But she was trying hard not to be one of them.

She folded her arms. "So why Oak Hills?"

He shrugged. "You'd have to ask my father. Clayton's the one who bought it."

Strange how he referred to his dad by his first name. She never did that with her family.

"Why are you here, then?"

The lines of his profile hardened. "Under orders."

"Under orders? As soon as your work is done, you'll move on to the next project?" She needed to make sure her plot for getting him out of Serenity Creek could work.

"More or less."

"Good. Let me know how I can help you on your way."

"Are you trying to get rid of me?" He feigned shock.

She mirrored his earlier answer. "Yes."

He laughed and bowed his head. "Well played."

The compliment warmed her inside, as did his rich voice. It was a sensation she refused to give into, since he was not only her enemy, but her client now as well.

He pulled off the dirt road they had been traveling on and parked under a large oak.

She looked around at nothing but mountainous forests of gnarled trees and bushy ferns. A small clearing marked the start of a trail she knew led to Serenity Creek, the curvy, rock-laden body of water from which the town derived its name.

Her last visit here had been more than a year ago when she was photographing the Oltens for their twentieth wedding anniversary. The day had started out warm with a slight breeze but by the time she had set everything up by the creek, gale force winds were blowing. At least they seemed gale force to her as they knocked over everything, including her, smack dab into the water and onto a pile of sharp rocks. She had walked away with bloody scrapes up and down her legs.

The time before that she had been photographing a proposal and the dark clouds overhead decided to let loose a torrential downpour right as the woman said yes and Madison had been about to capture the perfect moment. They had fled for their cars, a good ways off, and she had tripped in the rain, managing to save her camera but not her pride or her ankle, getting up covered in mud and limping.

No wonder she hated the outdoors. The forces of nature cost her a lot of time, money, and trouble. Even photographing an outdoor wedding would be easier than what she was going to be doing for Jake. With a wedding, dozens of people ran around making sure all went according to plan instead of only her keeping things in line.

She sighed and grabbed her camera bag. "I'm taking pictures of trees, then?"

"And other things. I'm told this is a popular spot with the locals, and there's a company in town that will arrange picnics, which we'll be trying later. You'll need these." He handed her a pair of hiking boots. "I'm guessing these are about right, but there are some other pairs in the back if you need a different size."

"How many pairs did you buy?"

"Enough to have a variety of sizes. I needed to make sure you had a good set of boots for today."

For the moment, the fact that today required boots was more concerning than his spending so much money on shoes just so she could have the right size.

She appraised the boots with disgust. "I think my sneakers will be fine." She felt her hold of the situation slipping through her fingers again.

"Not where we're going."

"You mean this isn't it?"

He shook his head. "We're hiking there."

"Excuse me?"

She had never traveled very far down the trail since she and nature obviously did not mix. It was too unpredictable and wild for her taste. She preferred to stay behind the lens and not get entangled with the wilderness.

She accepted the hiking boots with shaking hands.

He handed her one of the backpacks. "There's room in here for your camera bag. It'll be easier than carrying them separately."

"Joy," she mumbled, slipping her camera into the backpack.

She put on the boots and slung the bag onto her shoulder to follow him out of the car.

"This way." He motioned for her to follow him.

She walked behind him on the outlined path, picking her way through branches reaching out to touch her. Dried leaves crunched under her feet and the scent of wildflowers traveled on the wind. The scene would have been peaceful if not for her heart banging against her ribs.

"You know, I thought I was going to be taking photos of the local areas, not experiencing the local areas with you." She negotiated around a small snake crawling on the dirt, holding her breath and hoping it wasn't dangerous. She knew nothing of reptiles except that she didn't care for them.

"How else did you expect to get the prints we need?" he asked, expertly negotiating a steep slope.

She hadn't really thought about it. She had assumed the job would be an easy array of landscape pictures, not action shots.

He extended his hand out to help her down.

She was in no position to refuse his help even though every ounce of her pride screamed at her to not accept it.

"You mentioned a whole slew of places you wanted covered. What other adventures are in store for me?"

He glanced at her. "All different kinds."

The sexy look in his eyes bespoke volumes. He pushed a branch to the side. "We'll discuss it over lunch."

"So, nothing good then."

He was like the nature around her. Infuriatingly uncontrollable.

She needed to find out more about her nemesis if she was going to discover a chink in his armor. She remembered the information she had gathered on Colt Enterprises.

"What was it like growing up in New York? I can't even imagine such a big city."

"I didn't live there until I was ten."

The temperature plummeted around them with the coolness in his voice.

She pressed further, needing to comprehend the sudden change in his demeanor. The more she could understand him, the better grasp she'd have of the situation. "Where did you live before that?"

"In a little suburb of Connecticut where I was born. A tiny speck on the map."

She stopped on the spot, shocked. He had spent his childhood in a small town? Well, not all of it. And from the appearance of things, the big city upbringing was what prevailed.

"What made you guys move?"

She saw his shoulders tense, witnessed the brief falter in his step. It seemed as if minutes passed in silence, not seconds.

He adjusted his backpack. "We're almost there, but the hike gets more difficult up ahead from what the concierge told me."

The hard edge to his words told her she had reached a dead end in their conversation. He wouldn't give her answers.

As much as she wanted to know what had happened to him, more than she cared to admit, his advisement about the upcoming trek took priority. She didn't remember much about the trail from her previous visits, so his assessment was probably far more accurate than hers. Not to mention that if someone with no fear of heights or nature was warning her, then she had better pay attention.

They faced a rocky hill, and she watched him grab onto certain stones to steady himself with ease and surety—neither of which she felt as she followed behind him, her left foot scratching against some loose pebbles. But she made it up, brushing dirt off her jeans.

"Nicely done," he complimented.

"Thanks."

She heard a muffled crash ahead as they broke through some overgrown bushes.

A small waterfall cascaded over jagged rocks into a meandering stream that curved around moss-covered boulders and trees. Colorful flowers abounded all around them as sunlight flickered in past the canopy of leaves.

"It's so beautiful here." She set her bag down. "We locals consider Serenity Creek's waterfall the most striking and romantic spot around. I haven't been here in ages."

"Locals don't want their picture taken at the most striking and romantic spot of all time, through all the land?"

His sarcastic tone reminded her of why this cynical city dweller had to leave. She cut him a dirty look. "Locals experience their most private and memorable moments here. They take their own pictures."

"And you never come here on your own?"

Heaving a great sigh, she said, "Nature and I compete for control, and I never win. This is nature." She swirled her finger around to encompass the area around them. "I give it proper respect and distance."

"Hate to lose, huh?"

"You have no idea."

"Better than you think, actually. So do I." He leaned forward. "I even beat nature most of the time."

She wrestled with the urge to slap the taunting grin off his handsome face. Not the most ladylike and professional of moves.

"I'll just take some pictures," she ground out.

"This isn't the place I want."

"What? There's more?"

"Yup. Come on."

"Slave driver," she mumbled, picking up her bag again. "Are you sure you don't want photos of this? I mean, it is our town's namesake and probably our biggest tourist draw along with our wines, what with the fairytale and all."

His eyebrows drew together. "Fairytale? Oh, yeah. I think the maid mentioned something about that in her ceaseless praise of this place. Romeo and Juliet-like stuff?"

"I can see you paid such great attention to her." She rolled her eyes, not sure if he didn't remember because he didn't see fit to engage a maid in real conversation or because he wasn't interested in the love story the town was built upon. "Yes, like Romeo and Juliet minus the tragic ending. Well, maybe. No one really knows what happened, but I'd like to think they wound up happy after all that drama. Their plaque is over there." She pointed to a rectangle glinting in the sunlight trickling through the canopy of tree branches, a small token the town had set up over a hundred years ago to commemorate the lovers and their connection to the creek. The simple words rested forever in her memory banks as they did for every person who lived within a twenty-mile radius of Serenity Creek: Eduardo and Aurelia. May they be at peace together always.

He glanced at the marker, standing still and silent, motioning for her to continue.

"Are you going to listen to me better than you did the maid?"

His lips turned up with a tiny smirk. "You're a lot younger and far prettier. I think you have better odds of holding my attention for a romantic fable."

Heat crept up her neck as she struggled to regain her focus on the story instead of the come hither look in his eyes. "Aurelia Graciela, the daughter of King Stefano Casvino, fell in love with Eduardo Lisandro, the son of one of the noble families."

"Casvino? Where's that?"

"It was a little country next to Spain known for their wines."

"Was? It fell off the map or something?"

If he was trying to get a rise out of her, it was working. "It incorporated into Spain in 1890, hotshot. Where were you in history class?"

"Not learning about infinitesimal, no longer existent countries like Casvino."

She shrugged. "Fine. Stick with the world wars and major powers. They suit you better anyway. So Aurelia and Eduardo fell in love, but bad blood between the families kept them apart. The political cauldron was hot and starting to boil in 1880 when talks of deposing the monarchy starting circling, since there was no male heir to the throne and some noble families believed an elected prime minister should lead parliament. Want to guess who led the opposing faction against the crown?"

"Eduardo's family?"

"Yup. His father. Points for you."

"Makes for a rocky relationship."

She nodded. "Especially when the queen finally conceived again in 1882. King Stefano died that same year and his opponents accused the queen of an illicit affair, even going so far as to say that the child she was carrying was not of the royal bloodline. Letters were produced associating her with another nobleman. She and Aurelia, along with this nobleman, barely escaped alive and came to the United States. Supposedly, some of her relatives had built lives in California years earlier, but who knows? She built Rancho de Serenidad and the town was built up around it a few years later in 1885."

"Wasn't this about the lovers, not the town? What happened to them?"

She frowned. "The town and the story are interwoven."

He grinned. "For all eternity, basking in the glorious rays of love and sunshine and … "

"Okay, I get the picture." She held up her hand. Being raised on this bedtime story and living in it made her a tad partial.

"Eduardo searched for Aurelia and finally found her. They met here, at this very creek, and ran away together. No one knows what happened to them after that, and the town is split between the optimists who lean toward happily ever after and the ones who figure in that time, with the loads of political and family baggage they had, they wouldn't have made it far."

"What do you think?"

She scrunched up her nose and decided on honesty. "I don't know how Aurelia could have been so selfish to leave behind her mother and infant brother to run off with some guy."

His eyebrows rose. "Even for love?"

"Family comes first." She crossed her arms. "Besides, they could have stayed together and lived here. They didn't have to go running off."

"And we're back where we started. Do you have any idea what living in this place with all that gossip and speculation about them would have been like?" He scratched the back of his head. "Tell me, did you study anything else in history class besides Casvino?"

"Everything else was boring."

He laughed, a molten, rich chuckle that wrapped itself tightly around her.

"So, pictures of the world-famous creek where the lovers had their not-so-secret rendezvous?" she asked, squashing the telltale thumping of her heart.

"Hardly world famous. Which is why we don't need it. People already know about the creek itself, and they come here for the hike and scenery, not a history lesson."

Her jaw dropped at his cold calculation, uncertain of his reasoning. Maybe the men, but not the women. Women flooded to the fountain in Serenity Square with coins symbolizing wishes of love and happiness. They purchased every picture, some of which she had taken on the rare occasion she came here, of the infamous creek. In the end, though, it didn't really matter what

Jake did or didn't want photos of as long as she got rid of him so her parents could go back to running their winery their way without some interloper dictating the shots.

"We're going to cross the brook over there, so be careful of the rocks. They're going to be slippery." He pointed to a spot with stones strewn haphazardly between the two sides of the river.

"Just so I know, does our hike get worse than this?" she asked.

It wasn't that she didn't appreciate the natural beauty around her or didn't want to get her hands dirty, it was that she had too great of an appreciation for the raw power of the environment far beyond her management.

He led the way to their makeshift bridge. "No, and this is nothing compared to other hikes I was looking at in the brochures. I wouldn't want to push too much adventure on you so soon." He winked at her.

She'd show him a thing or two about her capabilities. Resentment made her double her steps.

She charged past him and set her foot on the first step, quickly taking the next.

"Take it slow, Madison," he warned behind her, all traces of his earlier jesting gone.

"I can take care of myself," she stated, speeding up. "I…"

Her foot slipped, striking the ice-cold water, sending her off balance. In an instant, she thought of the boulders around her and prayed her head wouldn't hit one as she fell, or her camera for that matter. She held her breath, waiting for impact, but instead of frigid water and craggy rocks, she hit strong, solid arms pulling her against a warm, muscled chest.

She gripped his shirt, still holding her breath as she stared up at Jake, concern etched in the lines of his face.

"I know you can take care of yourself, but sometimes it's nice to let someone else help you for a change."

He spoke with a calmness that contrasted directly with the heavy beating of his heart against her palm.

For one crazy moment, she wondered what it would be like to feel his lips on hers.

Whoa, where did that come from? Space. She needed space. She untangled herself from his grasp. "Thanks. Um, we should probably get going."

"Are you sure you're okay? Does your ankle hurt?" He started to lean down to inspect her sopping wet foot.

She moved away, careful to mind her surroundings this time. "I'm fine, really. Lead the way."

The look he sent her confounded her understanding of the man. It was at once a mixture of doubt, desire, and disquiet.

She squared her shoulders, shook her wet foot, and marched on behind him.

After another hour-long uphill hike, they reached a clearing and a grass-covered cliff. All around them birds flew through the bright, blue sky, and deep, green valleys spread out beneath them. A sweetly scented breeze wafted around them and the peaceful quiet of seclusion enveloped them.

She stood in awe of the splendor around her.

He spread out his arms to encompass the view. "Wasn't it worth it?"

In all honesty, she didn't know, and her answer had nothing to do with the walk and everything to do with her response to his earlier embrace. But she couldn't very well tell him.

"I guess so." She shrugged, pulling out her camera.

He cocked his head to the side.

"All right, all right. Yes," she gave in.

He nodded once. "Thank you."

She smiled back at him before lining up her first shot. "So what are you going to do with these shots? What media outlets are you going to use? Or are those details also reserved for lunchtime? It'll help me to know so I can plan the right photos."

"We'll be using a variety of different promotional material. Brochures for the regional hotels, an updated website for Oak Hills, national and local magazine advertisements."

She had to admit his strategy seemed sound. Tessa had done similar marketing for her family's winery with a fair amount of success, but Madison's parents had never been able to afford such robust advertising. But could he actually pull it off? And what would such a widespread campaign really mean for the winery?

He set his backpack down. "Anything I can do to help?"

She clicked off multiple pictures rapidly before moving to another part of the beautiful scene around them.

"Yes, actually," she said, still behind her camera. "You can stand over by that bush with your bag so I can get a shot of you."

"I don't do photo shoots."

His hard tone made her pull her camera down.

"What are you talking about? It'll be good to have a person in some of these images."

He shook his head. "Just like you don't fly, I don't do photographs."

She quirked up one of her eyebrows. She had encountered camera shy people before, but the rigid set of his jaw and relentless look on his face told her there was more to his story. "Is there a particular reason for that?"

"The paparazzi take more than enough pictures of me to last a lifetime. All accompanied by wonderful headlines about my so-called playboy, trust fund baby lifestyle."

A sliver of guilt shimmied through her as she had labeled him the same thing. "And you're not?" she asked, keeping her voice light. "Your economical bed is empty every night?"

He frowned. "I do date women, and yes, there have been many, but it's mutually agreed between the two of us that it's a fling and nothing more. I'm not ready to settle down and neither are the women I go out with. The terms are made clear in the beginning."

"So you're not a playboy, you just have commitment issues?"

He guzzled down water, pointing the bottle at her. "What about you? A beautiful woman like you still single leads me to believe you also aren't ready for the big walk down the aisle."

"Like I said, you don't know anything about me."

"I know you're not dating anyone or you wouldn't have been free for dinner last night." A smug smile played on his lips, which raised her hackles, and she met his sultry gaze head on.

"No, I'm not seeing anyone. I haven't found anyone more fulfilling than my photography. My *business* is my focus right now."

He whistled. "Talk about commitment issues. You're committed to the wrong thing, sweetie."

She huffed in frustration. "I wouldn't expect a fun-loving, irresponsible man like you to understand. And please stop calling me by little endearments. This is a professional relationship."

"I'm sorry. I didn't know that was part of the contract."

"It is."

He nodded, a dash of trouble about him. "I'll do my best."

She hid behind her camera again before he caught a glimpse of the unsettling effect his flirtatious teasing had on her.

"Do you have what you need? We should head back soon so we can make it to the car for lunch. I have the perfect spot picked out for a picnic."

A knot formed in her belly at the thought of hiking back. "Almost done. I hope you packed a large lunch because I'll be starving."

He chuckled, standing on the edge, staring out at the view. "You and me both."

She lined up her last shot. She couldn't help herself and he wouldn't notice. Angling the camera just right, she snapped a quick picture of his profile.

She had never met a man more unsettling than Jake Colt. She was hungry all right, but not for food. And that was the most disastrous truth of all.

# CHAPTER FIVE

Everything was perfect, just as Jake had planned. Fresh mountain air filled his lungs and a smorgasbord of food lay before them. Sunlight covered the spirited woman beside him while soft shadows played across her face from the shade of the trees. She was the best part of the whole package and the one thing not going as predicted.

He tasted the Oak Hills chardonnay the concierge had packed for them. He saw why the Carmichaels had chosen such a name for their winery; oak trees were widespread in this area.

"This is very good. Your father knows what he's doing. Now we need to make sure everyone knows it."

She drew her brows together. "Is this the first time you've tasted the wine you now own?"

A hint of guilt crept upon him. "Yes."

"Figures," she mumbled, sampling a slice of Jarlsberg cheese. "Where is this from anyway?" She motioned to the picnic spread before them.

"Tasty Treats. I talked to them about Oak Hills recommending their catering services to its customers and them recommending Oak Hills wine to theirs. When appropriate, of course."

He had hoped his efforts would win him some esteem from Madison, yet her face remained stern as she lowered her gaze and silently kept eating. Not an easy woman to please. He would have been disappointed had she been anything else, though.

The thrill in her eyes when he'd caught her in front of the waterfall still shot all sorts of creative thoughts through his mind. The sweet feel of her in his arms as he held her close lingered in his body.

She might be incredibly stubborn, but he was incessantly persistent. Especially when it came to something he wanted.

"Tell me about you. What got you interested in photography?"

He reached for a slice of freshly baked baguette at the same moment she went for a strawberry, her fingers brushing the back of his hand.

She withdrew quickly. "I can't remember a time when I wasn't interested in it. My parents gave me my first camera when I was six, and I instantly started snapping away even if it was just a toy. That wasn't my best work, mind you."

Maybe not, but he'd bet she still had them tucked away somewhere.

"I found myself spending more and more time taking pictures of the grapes instead of working with them alongside my dad."

A frown tilted her lips—what caused the change in her emotions?

She forged on. "And that's how I got started. Eventually, I went to the Brooks Institute and my work improved drastically from those first shots."

If he remembered correctly, the Brooks Institute resided less than an hour or so down the highway.

"You've stayed close to home."

She shrugged. "I like it here. Why wouldn't I stay?"

"You could probably find a lot more work in a city."

"Cities aren't that great."

He whistled. "Yes, they are. Fine dining, culture, opportunities of every kind."

"Pollution, crowds, crime. No, this is home. All of my family and friends are here, and I think we established that flying and traveling aren't my thing. I couldn't bear being away from them. And, though I don't appreciate being in the middle of the wild outdoors, no one can argue the photo ops in this area are amazing."

"I can't fathom being in one place for that long, particularly such a small place like this town."

And especially so near relatives. The thought made him shudder.

She must have seen the bewildered look on his face because she held her head high the way he had seen her do when he had unintentionally offended or angered her, something that happened more than his ego cared to admit.

"And what's wrong with this town? Have you even seen Rancho de Serindad?"

"The founding family's place? What was their name … Gracias?"

"Graciela. And yes, it's their place. The whole town was only named after it. No big deal."

"I thought it was named after the creek."

She rolled her eyes. "Serenidad is Spanish for serenity and the creek was nearby so they named the creek and the town Serenity Creek."

"I'm sorry. I didn't realize I was supposed to know the history of every miniscule town in America."

"You could at least know the history behind the town you've invested in."

"I haven't invested anything. Clayton has, and he bought your mom and dad's winery, not the town it's in."

"But wine and Serenity Creek have been intertwined since the beginning. The Graciela family planted the first vineyard in the area."

"Did they make a lot of money? Because then it would be good to spend our time exploring their wine-making and selling practices." He couldn't help but taunt her, seeing as how he hadn't faced a worthy opponent in a long time, besides his father, and Jake hated any interaction with that man.

She narrowed her eyes in an angry glare. "It's all about the money, isn't it? And what about you? Where did you get your business prowess from?"

He hated the corporate world, but he had been trained in it.

"I went to Harvard Business School," he answered in a straightforward manner.

She drank her wine. "Of course, you did."

A trickle of annoyance slipped through him. "You think Clayton got me in? He did push for Harvard and smoothed over the path, but I had the academics to get in by own merit."

College had been his favorite time in life. The schoolwork had been easy for him and he'd desperately needed the space from Clayton. He hadn't seen his father, not even on holidays, except for when he had been summoned to the office or the senior Colt had been invited to speak in one of his classes. He would have rather sat through a talk on the anatomy of locusts than hear his father's lectures.

Madison pulled her knees up in front of her, cradling her wineglass. "So what did you do when you graduated?"

"I traveled all over the place. Europe, Asia, South America. Europe beats out every place I've been to. I go there as often as I can."

"No, I mean what did you do for work? You know, what the rest of us lowly people do with our lives."

He flinched. "Clayton made me VP in his company. Why do you always emphasize the financial difference between us?"

She sputtered. "Because it's a huge difference."

He witnessed the deep, disapproving grooves forming on her face.

"Everything's been handed to you your whole life. School, a vice president title, cars, planes. What have you ever had to work for?" She set her glass down and swung her legs around, leaning forward.

He shifted his position, not quite sure where this was going. "I did have to do pretty well in school to get into Harvard, you know."

"I have no doubt about your intelligence. I think you possess a great many skills, but have you ever really applied them?"

He rested back against the trunk of the tree behind him, at a loss for words. No one had pointed out such a simple truth to him before. No one had cared about him enough to do so. The women in his life hadn't seen past his money or power to who he was beneath the surface.

He rubbed the back of his neck. He hadn't done anything for himself. He'd climbed, sailed, and skied all over the world, but those were enjoyments for him and him alone, an escape.

He wondered what she would think if she knew how much of a figurehead position he held. But he had no interest in Colt Enterprises. He didn't know what he wanted to dig his fingers into, he only knew he didn't want to work in an office with Clayton—whether that meant a commercial project in Hong Kong or a residential investment in Sydney didn't matter.

He scratched his head. "I don't have an answer for you."

She lowered her long lashes. "I'm sorry I asked such a rude question."

"Don't be, it's an honest one."

He could use more honesty in his life in a cutthroat, corporate world full of lies and deceit. Her sincerity tasted tantalizingly refreshing.

She raised her gaze to him again and he captured her stare.

They watched each other amid the soft sounds of the nature around them. He took in her lips, parting for an extra breath, his own respiration irregular.

He almost reached his hand to her when she cleared her throat and pulled back to grab the bottle of chardonnay.

"More wine?" she asked.

He gave her the space she obviously required despite his yearning to touch her again. "Sure."

She refilled his glass before studying the label. "This would make a great picture."

She set the bottle next to the spread of cheeses, positioning it so the front faced her. Lying on her stomach, she focused her camera and snapped shots in rapid succession, rotating to take pictures from different angles.

He thoroughly enjoyed watching her express her talent.

"So did the queen have an affair?"

She looked up from her camera. "Excuse me?"

"Aurelia's mother. You said she was accused of having an affair. Did she?"

She shook her head, her shoulders sagging. "No one knows for sure. She gave birth to a son, but nothing was ever proven as to who fathered the child. It's not like they could just run a DNA test or something in that time."

"What about descendants? Are there any still in town?"

Fairytales, real or make believe, didn't interest him, but he couldn't stop himself from asking more questions. She obviously had some reservations about the story and didn't buy into it 100 percent, but every word she spoke held such passion for this town she had grown up in, for the family she loved. It was a passion he had never experienced outside of an adrenaline rush.

She scrunched up her nose. "Not anymore. Descendants of Aurelia's half brother, Renato, used to live in town but Widow Graciela's children left when her husband died. My mom used to visit her with pies and casseroles. I don't think her family ever came back. Mom said it was hard for any Graciela living in Serenity Creek, with all the speculation and gossip constantly going around."

A deep, dark resentment flared in his gut like a deadly poison. He could relate all too well to the Gracielas, remembering the cruel, calculating gossip-mongering that he himself had to endure in the backward town he had once called home. When he had most needed kindness, he had been met with selfish rumors and opportunistic residents looking for a quick buck.

The click of Madison's camera as she took another picture of the picnic dragged his mind back to the present. "Did Mrs. Graciela live at Rancho Serenidad?"

She nodded. "Widow Graciela. She would smack your head if you called her Mrs. Graciela. At least she used to when she actually went out. In her later years, she just remained holed up in the house, and that's when Mom brought her food." She snapped a few more shots of the area around them, not once looking at him. "She took me with her once to the Rancho. It was just as huge and extravagant inside as it was outside. Empty feeling, though."

"Who's there now?" He brushed a recently fallen tree leaf from his shoulder.

"No one. It's been vacant since Widow Graciela passed away. I think her granddaughter owns it now. Why? Are you interested in buying it, too?" She paused a moment in her work to scowl at him.

"Not really."

Not even a little. Another piece of dirt in Small Town, USA? No, thanks. He just liked hearing Madison talk to him rather than always cutting him with her cold looks and blatant criticism. This quaint little story seemed to keep her going.

"Good, because that's the last thing Serenity Creek needs."

He put a hand over his chest. "I'm hurt. You mean you don't want me buying a house and moving in permanently?"

She zeroed in on him, shooting imaginary darts at his head, no doubt—the glare that could slice through steel.

"So what other adventures do you have in mind? And how fast can we get them over with?" she asked, scooting forward and lining up a shot of the oak trees behind them.

He grinned. She wasn't going to like his idea, but he needed to loosen her up. Someone had to and he definitely wanted the job. "They're a surprise. I'll pick you up for the shoots and take you to the locations."

Her jaw dropped. "I can't work under those conditions. I have to be able to organize my supplies, my schedule, my life."

He relaxed back against a tree trunk, taking another sip of wine and enjoying every minute of her increasing discomfort. "Yes, what would you do if your whole day wasn't coordinated down to the last second?"

"I have to understand what you have arranged."

"Nope."

She pointed her finger at him. "If you want me to take pictures for you, I need to be involved."

"You're free to walk away from this if you want. I can hire another photographer, find someone who comes highly recommended from LA. The choice is yours." He loved calling her bluff.

She set her hands on her hips and straightened her back as if pure determination ignited her whole body. This was where he could relate to her, in the will to fight.

•••

Madison watched the look of certainty fill Jake's eyes from across the picnic blanket.

She hated giving him exactly the answer he wanted and had expected, but she hated backing down even more.

She threw up her hands. "Fine. You win. This time. I'll go along with your crazy surprise adventure scheme."

He winked. "I won't let you down, sweetheart."

She couldn't stand the way her nerves buzzed every time he used an endearment. "If you call me sweetheart one more time, I'm going to do something to prove to you I'm not that sweet."

"Oh, I know you're not that sweet." He raked his eyes from the top of her head to her curling toes.

The man was intolerable. Gorgeous, but intolerable. She'd go along with his silly plan, but only long enough to kick his city slicker butt back to New York where it belonged, thousands of miles away.

"I can meet you at the winery tomorrow since you'll be there with my dad. We'll need to get some shots of it. The vineyards, the tasting room, the cellar … " She stopped at the confused look on his face. "You are going to be at the winery with my dad tomorrow, right?" He squirmed. The overly confident, always sure of himself man squirmed. And his answer was written in his downcast eyes.

He had never intended to work with her father tomorrow.

She massaged her temple. "I don't understand. What are you doing tomorrow if you're not going to be working at the winery? You're the new owner. I thought that was the reason you're here."

"I hadn't really thought about tomorrow's schedule with the winery."

No, but he definitely had all of his mysterious adventures planned out. Typical. The guy was an adrenaline junkie and couldn't be bothered with something so mundane as actual work.

On the one hand, that meant he wouldn't be getting in the way of her father's decisions. On the other, the longer he took to get his work done, the longer he would be here, and that was just unacceptable on all levels.

Frustration clawed at her. "Are you even taking this seriously?"

His jaw set and darkness crossed his eyes. "I'll be there tomorrow. You can count on it."

She doubted it. Her family's pride and joy, their dream, rested in this man's irresponsible hands. Not for long if she had anything to say about it.

She tucked her hair behind her ear. "I won't hold my breath."

He caught her wrist, leaning in close, his eyes as bottomless as the ocean depths. "Madison, trust me. I promise I won't let you down. Not with Oak Hills and not with our marketing strategy."

Her pulse jumped under his thumb.

She had seen it in the shocked look on his face, the tensing of his shoulders. He had never intended to help her father, to do anything for Oak Hills besides what served his purposes. She wanted him gone, but she didn't want him to take the winery down with him. Something else stared back at her now in his eyes, though. Hard, unrelenting determination.

Trusting him could prove to be a fatal mistake. Right alongside allowing herself to fall for a guy who had never worked a day in his life and thrived on a fast paced, jet-setting lifestyle. Neither was an option.

• • •

Later that night, Madison sat at her two-person oak table off her miniscule kitchen, poring over her budget and financial projections for her business. Good thing Tessa would be over soon for dessert, because her current task kept sinking her deeper into a depressing mood with each swipe of her calculator. She needed chocolate and her best friend. Desperately.

Numbers stared up at her, telling her a story she didn't want to hear. She needed Jake's job. She couldn't survive without it, yet she couldn't very well live with the whole town thinking she and Jake were dating.

She sighed. She'd get the job done, put the crazy rumors to rest, and then she needed to capitalize on the publicity she would gain by doing such a large-scale project for Oak Hills and the surrounding area.

She sat down at her laptop to work on the spreadsheet she had started for her own marketing purposes. The cursor blinked back at her, waiting for her to type her next inspired idea. Nothing came. She couldn't focus. Her thoughts kept straying back to the handsome face that was both the cause of all her trouble and her one way out of it.

Her doorbell chimed, interrupting her daydream of Jake and their hike earlier today. This time, she peeked out the tiny window next to the door to make sure it wasn't Mrs. Tobin again before opening it. Or Jake. Why he would stop by she didn't know, but she did know her heart gave a funny flop at the thought.

Tessa stood outside laden with goodies.

Madison opened the door and motioned her in. "You have great timing. If I had to look through my financial statements one more time, you would have found me banging my head against the wall, literally."

"That bad, huh?"

"I can't talk about it until I have chocolate in me."

Tessa lifted her treasure-filled arms. "I can definitely help you there. *Nonna* made us her famous tiramisu, and I brought a bottle of Oak Hills Pinot Noir for good measure."

Madison walked the two steps it took to reach the couch and coffee table. "You could have brought a bottle of your Gianini wine."

"I wanted to support your family in any way I can."

"Thank you." Madison took the plastic container from Tessa and set it on the table. "I love your grandmother. She's amazing. Doubly so for making tiramisu when I'm in desperate need of something sinfully delectable."

Tessa giggled. "I'll let her know you appreciate her talents."

"Go ahead and sit. I'll get the glasses, plates, and forks."

Madison strode into the kitchen to gather the necessities.

"Sorry I was late. We had a family meeting to discuss upcoming harvest celebrations," Tessa said.

"That must have been fun."

"You have no idea." Tessa nestled into the couch. "I had heard a few whisperings that you and Jake were out and about together. More than once."

Madison eyed her.

Tessa put her hand to her chest. "I'm trying to squelch such rumors, of course."

"Thank you. Because they're completely unfounded."

"Completely, huh?" Tessa accepted the glasses Madison held out to her.

"Yes." She frowned as she lit the row of rose-scented candles arranged on the fireplace mantle, taking in her favorite, comforting smell. "Why do you ask?"

Tessa shrugged. "Oh, I don't know. I heard you two were spotted at The Wine Cork over a romantic candlelit dinner and something about a hike and picnic lunch being arranged for both of you. Sounds like a bit more than business."

"I'm taking photographs for him to use in a marketing strategy for the winery so I can help Mom and Dad, get him out of here, and keep my own dream going in the process. It's just a means to an end."

Tessa expertly uncorked the wine like the winemaker she was and poured them each a glass. "I understand, but you're telling me you're not the least bit tempted?"

Madison faltered. She didn't lie, especially not to her best friend.

Tessa zeroed in on her misstep. "You are."

Madison took a large gulp of wine. "Maybe a little. But I know it's not a good thing, and I refuse to indulge such ludicrous fantasies."

Madison cut large slices of tiramisu and put them on the small, white plates she had snatched earlier, handing one to Tessa.

"No one can blame you for being interested. I saw him. He's hot." Tessa swirled her wine as if it were second nature, breathing in its bouquet before taking the first sip.

Madison took a bite of the dessert, savoring its fluffy, coffee-tinged taste. "I can't deny he's gorgeous. It's the rest of him that's a problem. The whole stealing my family's winery, robbing me of my much needed business, rich, lofty attitude, city thing."

"I ran a credit check on the guy."

"What? How?" Madison asked, her words garbled over the large piece of tiramisu in her mouth.

"I went through the third party we use for background checks on winery employees."

Madison swallowed hard. "Why didn't I think of doing that?"

A sly look flashed across Tessa's face. "Because you're not nearly as sneaky as I am."

"Maybe I should take lessons."

"Why, when I can do the sneaky stuff for you? Do you want to know what I found out?"

Like she could resist.

"Of course, what kind of question is that?"

Tessa laughed. "Nothing big. At least, nothing we didn't already know. He appears genuinely loaded. Although, everything seems to be in his father's name or the corporation's name, not Jake's."

"So his dad holds the purse strings. I'm sure Jake gets a pretty penny from Colt Enterprises as a VP."

"Oh, he does. Trust me. The man is very well paid from what I gathered in my research."

What exactly did Jake do for that money? Fly around and climb mountains?

"There's something else I saw when I looked him up online," Tessa said, her words slow and careful.

Madison knew where this was going. Jake had admitted his affinity for the opposite sex already, but it still grated on her nerves. "I know all about … "

"Not that it matters," Tessa jumped in quickly.

"Oh, it matters. His dating record reads like a who's who of the international social scene. Models, actresses, heiresses. He's way out of my league, just like Tucker was."

The corners of Tessa's lips quirked up. "I thought you didn't care because you weren't interested. And for the record, you were out of Tucker's league, way out. The guy should have been upfront with you from the beginning."

"I agree with you there." Madison clinked her wine glass against Tessa's. "And you're right. I don't care and it doesn't matter. Jake Colt can date whomever he wants because it sure won't be me. We're in a business relationship, nothing more."

She wished her words sounded stronger.

# CHAPTER SIX

Jake knew two things. One, keeping his promise to Madison and spending the day at the winery was the right decision. And two, working in the vineyards on a glorious, sunny morning beat the office any day.

"I'm happy you've taken such a keen interest in how our wine is made, Jake. Some people might take an uncaring, bottom line only approach," Thomas said, leading them through the neatly arranged rows of grapes.

He could tell from the undercurrent in Thomas's tone that he had thought Jake would take the indifferent route. Normally, he would be right, but Madison's words yesterday had spurred something in Jake, compelling him to take a deeper look at Oak Hills.

"It's good to know a business from the inside out," Jake responded, crouching down on the ground next to Thomas in front of a vine.

"This is where it all starts. Right here, with the grapes and the soil." Thomas lifted some dirt and shook it through his fingers.

This could be a very long day if Thomas's beginning was anything to go by. He had time to kill, though, since Madison wouldn't be arriving for another few hours.

"If your soil is good that's half the battle. We're blessed with that and great weather, warm days and cool nights. These little beauties love it." Thomas held a plump grape bunch with a gentle touch.

"Can't blame them. I'd thrive in this weather, too."

As long as it came with a big city and some sky diving and skiing. But he couldn't deny the exquisite sense of peace that enveloped him in the quietness of the vineyard. A far cry from the usual noise he enjoyed.

Thomas rose and led them further down the aisle, telling him more about the soil conditions, trellising, and how to know when the grapes were ready for harvest.

What shocked Jake more than anything was his desire to hear more. The passion lighting up the man's voice enticed him to know what caused such a reaction.

"I've never been an office type. I can't stand being inside for very long." Thomas walked ahead toward the single building that housed the tasting room, cellar, and offices all under one roof. "We won't spend much time in here."

Jake paused, his curiosity piqued. "I'm the same way."

Thomas stopped at the doorway, cocking his head to the side. "Really? I thought you spent most of your time in an office, being a VP and all."

Truthfully, he saw little of the corporate building and that was still too much for him. "I get out as much as I can."

Thomas nodded. "I completely understand. I'm so glad Rose handles the administration details so I can focus on the wines. She's a treasure, that one."

"You're very lucky."

• • •

The last sight Madison expected to see stood before her: Jake laughing it up with her dad over glasses of wine outside the tasting room at Oak Hills. How had her sensible little world been so completely dismantled?

Worse yet, somehow the scene seemed natural, as if Jake belonged right next to her dad at the winery. It was as pleasurable as her attraction to Jake and just as ill conceived and traitorous.

He was the enemy. He had no place in her life or in her family's lives and she would do well to remember it.

The door on her Toyota moaned in protest as she slammed it shut and slipped her camera strap over her neck, marching up to the two men. A large flash of fur rushed past her as Cork raced up to Jake, tail wagging. The dog curled up at his feet, savoring every pat, scratch, and rub Jake gave out.

She shook her head, seriously concerned with Cork's total and complete lack of good judgment when it came to character. Then again, he was only a dog. What was her excuse?

Well, Cork could cater to the man all he wanted. She wouldn't bow down to his incessant charm, no matter how good the man's touch felt.

"Having a fun time, are we?" she asked, folding her arms in front of her.

"Your dad's been showing me the ropes around here." Jake motioned with his now empty wine glass.

Thomas slapped him on the back. "I think this boy has great potential. We'll make a winemaker out of him yet."

She had no doubt about his off-the-charts potential. He had gone to Harvard for crying out loud and smoothly handled anything life threw at him. But he squandered his talents in the wrong places, mainly women and boyish adventures.

"Jake's not staying around that long," she said sweetly.

"I could surprise you."

"I don't think so."

She wouldn't be falling for that lie again any time soon. Tucker had taught her well: city folk always remained city folk no matter what they professed.

"I've been doing it a lot lately."

She plunked her hands on her hips. "Are you ready?"

Thomas finished off his wine. "I should get back to my tasting notes. I'll take these." He grabbed Jake's wine glass as Cork rose to follow him inside. "You two play nice, now."

Her dad sent her a warning glance as he turned back to the building, but she didn't miss the look he sent Jake as well. She wasn't the only one being told to behave.

She spun away from Jake's amused stare and strode toward the vineyards.

He caught up with her.

"That's not your actual car, is it?" He hitched his thumb over his shoulder to her beat-up four-door.

"I drove up in it, didn't I? I'm not sure how many cars you have, but I only have that one."

"That doesn't count as one, it's more like a half."

She fought the laughter bubbling up in her and shrugged. "It runs."

"Barely. You need a new one."

She snorted. "Not all of us can afford whatever our heart desires. My car is fine."

"I can give you an advance for the work you're doing. We haven't talked about a timeline for payment."

Annoyance crackled through her. "Half now, half upon completion. That's my standard contract and that's what we're sticking with. Even the entire payment won't cover the cost of a new car. Not to mention I'll be using that money for other things, mainly my photography."

And mostly in solidifying it. But she didn't want him to know how desperate her business finances were, or her own.

"I can throw in a bonus for having to deal with an unplanned schedule I know you hate."

The man was an unstoppable force, used to getting whatever he wanted or decreed. But not with her.

"No. For the last time, no. Let's move on. We have work to do. Are there any particular pictures you need?"

"What happened to playing nice?"

She glared at him. "Went out the window when you insulted my car. Anything you specifically want out here before we move inside?"

He raked his stare over her body. "Definitely."

She cleared her throat, fumbling with her camera. "I'll just take a variety of photos."

She adjusted her lens, lining up a shot of the vines and providing a nice barrier between them. She took a few pictures in silence as he examined some grapes. Her curiosity got the best of her. "So what did you talk about with my dad?"

"You."

"Excuse me?"

He strolled up alongside her. "Only for a little bit. Your dad spent the morning teaching me about how he blends his varietals and what the process entails. I have to admit I was amazed at how passionate he is about this place and the wine he makes here."

"It's his dream. I have so much respect for him and my mom, developing Oak Hills from the ground up. They worked hard to achieve what they knew they were meant to do for the rest of their lives."

She watched as he walked ahead of her a few steps, towering over the grapevines like his demeanor towered over everything within his sphere of influence. And what a big sphere it was, encompassing her life and her family's. "That is, until you swooped in to commandeer and destroy everything they've built."

He froze and slowly turned around, his jaw set in a hard line. "No, I came here to save what they built."

He looked away from her before moving down the aisle, tension radiating from his broad shoulders to his purposeful pace.

Maybe she had taken things too far. He had shown up today and spent time with her dad as he had promised. But her gut told her he had little interest in real employment or helping her parents. Still, she may have been a tad harsh.

He brought out the worst of her obstinate, aggressive attitude she usually kept in check.

He knelt down in front of a grape bunch, handling it with care as he tested their firmness with a gentle squeeze. Apparently, he had learned a lot in the last few hours.

She brought her camera up, zooming in on him, bringing the shot into focus. What she saw in the lens took her breath away.

For the first time, she caught a glimpse of what truly existed under his playboy shield. She distinguished the sharp intelligence etched into the lines of his face, the softness in the tender touch of his hands, and the deep hurt engraved in his cobalt blue eyes.

What great things would this man be capable of when he set his mind to it? What had caused the entrenched pain emanating from him? It had to be something more than her comment.

The ice around her heart began to thaw.

He rotated in her direction and she clicked off the shot.

"Sorry, I couldn't resist," she said, her throat thick.

He rose, sending her a sexy smile, but his movements toward her belied something more serious. "I'm glad you've finally admitted you can't resist me."

She fumbled with her camera strap. "Don't flatter yourself."

He stopped inches from her. "Have dinner with me tonight at the hotel. To discuss the promotional plan."

She hesitated.

"And as a way for you to make amends for the unauthorized picture you just took," he said, a teasing quality to his voice.

Best not to tell him about the photograph she took yesterday. What would she be required to do to make up for that one?

"All right. What time?"

"Say seven?"

"Sure."

Warning sirens sounded in ears. She was supposed to get rid of the guy, not fall for him. Where would that leave her when she succeeded and he left?

• • •

Jake pored over the financial statements for Oak Hills in the stillness of his hotel room, the early evening sun seeping through the windows. He sipped some of his coffee, scrunching his face as he realized it had gone cold.

He couldn't get the winery, the grapes, the harvest, or the soil off his mind. He had spent the last couple of hours scouring every document he had on Oak Hills; he had put in several calls around town and one to the corporate office for his secretary, Nancy Olton. She was the only person he trusted in that lion's den his father considered a workplace and one of the only constants in his life, even if she did overstep her bounds when it came to certain decisions he made. Sometimes she acted more like his mother than an employee, or even a friend.

The shock in Nancy's voice had temporarily halted her efficiency. His in-depth questioning and the amount of research he asked her to gather for him was a far cry from his usual requests for plane tickets and hotel reservations. Investing his all into a project was a new notion.

He hated that part, playing right into Clayton's manipulation for him to take an active role in a company he had no interest in. But he wasn't doing this for his father or Colt Enterprises. He had made a promise to Thomas and Madison to see this through and maintain the dignity of the winery, and he intended to keep it.

No small task considering Clayton would battle him on it every step of the way. In Clayton's mind, bigger was always better. He would want to transform Oak Hills into a large-scale production.

Jake leaned back in the antique dark wood chair, massaging his sore neck. He had developed a more extensive marketing strategy that centered on a promotional sweepstakes and would highlight the quality and exclusivity of the wine. He could run it by Thomas when he met with him tomorrow to discuss harvest plans.

He rubbed his eyes. It felt good to dig into the inner workings of the winery, get his hands dirty in the soil of the vineyard. He wanted to get involved beyond promotions and finances to the heart of Oak Hills, a concept he had never experienced before. But he was here on a temporary pass and he refused to get attached to anything. He'd do this job and then hit the Alps, the faster the better, before old memories of the other small town he had lived in, the one he had grown up in, became more than he could bear.

But the idea of leaving Madison behind left a sour taste in his mouth.

It had to be because she refused every single one of his charms. And he couldn't forget her sultry curves, good looks, and razor-sharp wit. He wouldn't leave without exploring the possibilities she held, starting with tonight.

He stared down at his notes. He had a choice. He could keep plugging away at his new plan for the winery while dwelling on thoughts of Madison, or he could get out and have some fun, or at least as much fun as this town allowed, which limited his options drastically.

He pushed away from the desk and headed to the closet for a change of clothes. He'd hit the streets for a run. Everything made more sense when he was exerting energy. The pavement would have to do for now. He'd get his thoughts straight. Then he'd shower and meet Madison for dinner.

# CHAPTER SEVEN

Jake stood at the base of the grand staircase in the hotel lobby, shifting his weight from foot to foot and fingering the single red rose in his hands, an impulse buy the concierge had helped him with.

He couldn't contain his nervous energy nor could he comprehend it. He'd been on a good deal of dates, taken many women out to dinner, so why was he anxious about this one?

His run had done nothing to clear his head. He had to get a grip on himself. The concierge had arranged everything with the restaurant and Madison would be here any minute. Nothing would go wrong. What woman didn't like being wined and dined in style?

The front door creaked open as Madison stepped in. Her simple black, sleeveless dress hugged her smooth curves, contrasting with the light color of her long hair curling past her shoulders.

She looked stunning. Never had he met a more enigmatic woman, all soft splendor on the outside, but a prickly temper on the inside.

She stopped in front of him. "Sorry, I'm late. My car wouldn't start."

"I'm serious about you needing a new one."

She blew out an exasperated breath and he could see the argument brewing in her eyes.

"Before you get all worked up, this is for you." He held out the rose to her. "You look beautiful."

Her hand wavered a little as she accepted the flower. She tucked her hair behind her ear, fidgeting. "Thanks."

At least he wasn't the only one a little edgy around here.

She brought the rose up to her nose, taking in its scent, the gesture feminine and sensual.

Yearning slithered through him. "Shall we?" He offered her his arm.

She took it and fell into step alongside him.

He led them into the hotel's finest restaurant, albeit their only restaurant and the most luxurious in town. All eight tables of it.

The maitre d' greeted them instantly. "Good evening, Mr. Colt and Miss Carmichael. Everything is ready for you."

They followed the suit-clad man around the sparse array of white linen, candlelit tables. The room buzzed with the gentle hum of conversation as more than a few eyes turned their direction.

"Here we are." The maitre d' indicated a secluded spot in the corner, sheltered somewhat by the dark mahogany paneling, but with a view of everyone.

Jake pulled out the chair for Madison before taking his own seat.

Madison set her flower next to her plate.

"Could you please bring us a glass of water for the lady's rose?" Jake asked.

"Of course, sir, right away."

"What?" he said at Madison's stunned expression.

"I didn't think you were into details like that," she answered.

"Then you have a lot to learn."

"If there is anything at all I can assist you with, Mr. Colt, please do not hesitate." The man walked away, one corner of his lips lifted in a half smile, and left the two of them alone.

"You have him trained. Are people always so accommodating for you?" Madison asked just as another waiter appeared with a silver bucket and some Dom Perignon champagne.

A second waiter came up behind him carrying a vase filled with water, which he placed near Madison before immersing the rose in it and scurrying off.

The other man presented the bottle to Jake. "As you requested, sir."

He poured each of them a glass before nestling the champagne back in the chilled container. "Your appetizer will be right out," he said, darting back to the kitchen.

She leaned forward, ignoring the expensive bubbles before her. "Why are there no menus in front of us?"

Jake sipped his champagne, his unease escalating. Had he made the right decision? This set up went over well with every woman he had ever taken out. "You made a comment at The Wine Cork about me ordering for you. I thought I would put it to the test." If he requested all the right items, what did it matter who actually initiated the selections?

"And you think that's going to go well for you?"

He leaned forward, his poker face locked in place. "I have no doubt."

"I do."

"I guess we'll have to see who's right."

She pinched the stem of her glass. "I don't recall Dom Perginon being on the menu here."

"I had it special ordered."

She furrowed her brow. "Is there anything you don't special order?"

"Try your champagne." He indicated her still untouched drink.

She tasted it.

"Well?" he asked.

She shrugged. "It's okay."

"Okay?"

"Yeah, it's okay."

He stared at her incredulously. He had spoiled many women with such luxurious treats and never had he received that response.

She must have perceived his shock because she explained, "I'm not really into champagne. I'm more of a wine gal and partial to California over France. It's too hoity-toity for me."

He recalled his plans for the rest of the extravagant feast and a drop of sweat slid down his back. Jake Colt sweating over a woman? He would have thought the notion ridiculous even an hour ago, but that was before Madison had walked into the lobby in that killer dress. A challenge was one thing, but she might prove impossible.

Their waiter appeared again, positioning a plate with succulent aromas wafting from it in between them. "Here are your crab cakes. Is there anything else I can get you right now?"

"No, that will be all. Thank you," Jake said. He made no move for the food and instead studied Madison. She perplexed him. The fancier the treat, the more lavish the setting, and the more money he spent on her, the colder she acted. She was actually turned off by his grand gestures, a fact he had trouble wrapping his head around.

On the other hand, she had zeroed in on the gaping gulf between their financial situations—he was starting to realize how different she really was from everyone else he had dated, and how special.

He had to switch gears if he was going to salvage the evening.

"I apologize. Perhaps you were right and I don't know you very well." He placed his hand over hers. "Why don't you help me change that?"

She stared at the point of contact for an instant and then scanned the room, looking over her shoulder. She turned back to him, biting her lower lip. "What do you want to know?"

Relief rushed through him. "Start with your favorite drink so I don't get that wrong in the future and go from there."

He saw her whole body go rigid and knew the exact word that had caused such a response, because the same word sent his pulse rate skyrocketing. Future. He, Jake Colt, had just said "future" to a member of the opposite sex.

"If we're talking wine, my family's chardonnay is my all time fave. The vintage a few years ago was beyond delicious." As she spoke, her shoulders relaxed and her tone turned casual, comfortable.

She went on to share about her mother's great cooking skills as she split up the appetizer between them.

He settled into the conversation, shocked to discover how much he enjoyed this simple act of talking with her. Where they were or what they were eating didn't matter—she did. More than he cared to admit.

For a guy who prided himself on not committing to anything, including relationships, the realization disturbed him deeply. He needed to proceed with caution or this game he had started could get a lot more serious, fast.

• • •

Madison sampled more of the overpriced champagne as she spoke about her mom's famous chocolate chip cookies.

She never felt comfortable in such expensive restaurants. She had no interest in anything more elaborate than The Wine Cork. Yet, somehow here she was, spilling her life story to a man she had sworn to hate. What was she doing?

She stopped talking as their main course of filet mignon with garlic mashed potatoes arrived.

She smirked. The meal fell right in line with the champagne and the rich, jet-setting man sitting across from her, highlighting what she already knew. They couldn't live in two more different galaxies. And yet, he didn't miss a beat of politeness with the staff, nor fail to be the perfect gentlemen with her.

She had almost written the evening off as a complete waste, but then he'd suddenly changed and shown a real interest in what she was saying, forgetting all the fancy fluff around them. She started to enjoy the smooth taste of the champagne, the succulent aroma of steak and potatoes.

Her gaze fell upon the rose. By far, it was the best part of the night. Simple, sweet, and too sexy for her personal well-being.

"What about you? Why do you like Europe so much?" she asked, clearing her mind of such dangerous thoughts.

"The night life, the skiing, the sailing, the architecture, the history, and every other excitement life offers," he answered easily.

Right. The man never worked. What did he do with all of his time besides play?

All the more reason she should smother the insane attraction for him growing within her. There was no future between them.

She opened her mouth to give him a piece of her mind, anything to keep from thinking about the way his tailored dove-gray suit perfectly fit his honed body or how his dark blue tie deepened the sapphire shade of his eyes.

A man striding up to them stopped her. She knew him by reputation to be the owner of the hotel.

"Bobby, I'm glad you could stop by," Jake greeted.

"Hello, Jake. I hope the dinner is to your liking." Bobby set his hand on Jake's shoulder.

Typical for a guy like Jake to be on a first-name basis with the owner of where he was staying. She wouldn't consider men of his stature appreciating being addressed so informally, though.

The fact that Jake did revealed a more humble side to him than she thought existed.

From the moment she had met him, she had been looking at him through her own jaded lens. Maybe it was time to switch it out for a better one, give him a fair assessment. But with great caution. Seduction was a way of life for this man, so discerning fact from fiction was crucial.

"Everything is perfect. Let me introduce you to Madison Carmichael. Madison, this is Bobby Shaw. He owns the Maple Grove Inn."

She shook hands with him. "It's nice to meet you."

"The pleasure is all mine. I've met you before if I recall correctly, but you were running around in pigtails then. You're all grown up now and quite a beaut." Bobby winked at Jake.

"That she is," Jake said, holding her gaze.

Madison slid lower in her seat, for once wishing not everyone around here had known her since she was born.

"I'm excited to be partnering with your family's winery in this new promotional sweepstakes." Bobby's plump, rosy cheeks bunched as he smiled.

"I know it means a lot to my parents to be collaborating with you on discounts and cross advertising," she said, enjoying the man's genuine joviality.

"I think it will be good and we're happy to promote Oak Hills with brochures in our rooms, but I'm more interested in this contest idea Jake's been talking to me about. I wouldn't trust another person to be able to pull something like this off."

She looked between the two men, at a loss for what he meant.

"I haven't had the chance to explain this new aspect of our marketing plan to her," Jake said easily. "We're going to review the details over dessert."

"Well, I won't keep you. I only wanted to stop by to say how delighted I am you would come to us with such an offer," Bobby said before his cell phone buzzed and he excused himself.

She stared at Jake, surprised he'd already been wheeling and dealing with local merchants. "What's going on?"

He chuckled. "Can't wait till dessert, huh?"

"Are you kidding?"

He shook his head. "Impatient as always."

"Eager. The term is eager. Why didn't you tell me earlier?"

"Pleasure before business."

His motto for life, but did he ever get around to the business end? Apparently he did if their conversation with Bobby Shaw was anything to go by.

"And I wanted us to talk about something other than the winery. I wanted to chat about you. At least for a little while," he added.

Her heart fluttered. She enjoyed sparring with him, being with him, but it was a slippery slope from the work category to the personal one, and they were on their way.

She clasped her glass, finishing off her champagne. "I'm ready to talk marketing now."

He refilled her flute. "I was thinking we need a fresh angle if we're going to bring in the size of clientele needed to financially jump-start Oak Hills. But I want to be careful not to destroy the small, boutique atmosphere of the winery."

Since when was he interested in preserving her father's vision? She didn't even think he understood it, but perhaps she had been wrong.

"How do you propose going about that?"

Their waiter ambled up to the table with a chocolate soufflé topped with a dollop of whipped cream, which he positioned between them. Despite the scent of warm, gooey chocolate she normally would have dug into with delight, she held back, impatiently waiting for Jake's response.

"We set up a sweepstakes where the grand prize is an all-inclusive trip here. It'll cover hotel stay, wines, food, excursions, everything. We'll print tickets on the back of Oak Hills wine bottles like when soda companies run contests, and we'll set up a place on the website where people can enter for free. The contest itself will drum up sales and give the winery, and the rest of the town, great exposure."

"But most people would buy the wine at their local stores, not at the winery, so sales would increase but not necessarily traffic flow." Her enthusiasm increased with each word, as did her respect for him.

"Yes, to an extent. I don't want you to think there won't be any expansion required at the winery, because demand will go up and we'll have to increase supply, not to mention the whole area will be promoted so more tourists will show up," he cautioned.

She nodded, dipping her spoon into the dessert. "I understand, as long as the expansion doesn't get out of hand."

"We'll keep it within reason."

Maybe she was wrong. Maybe he did put in an effort. He had certainly performed wonders with the owner of the Maple Grove Inn.

But Jake was still an interloper. History had taught her men like Tucker looked out only for themselves, so Jake required close supervision to make sure things didn't get out of control. It was a task she was all too thrilled to handle, which created an even bigger problem than his interference in the winery.

She couldn't fall for a rich, famous playboy. She refused to be just another one of his conquests. The guy wouldn't stick around long enough to kiss her goodbye when all this was done. And that's what she wanted, right? This to be done and him to be gone.

Confusion and champagne muddled her senses as they finished dinner. So much so that she didn't notice Ava Gianini approaching them until it was too late.

"Just shoot me now," she mumbled under her breath.

"What?" Jake asked.

"Nothing. We have a visitor," she whispered.

Ava stopped in front of their table, shifting an inquisitive glance between the two of them. "Madison, it's so good to see you out and about. As soon as I sat down with my friends," she pointed to a table with three ladies all staring at them, "and saw you, I knew I had to stop by."

Not really. Madison didn't see any reason for the visit except to meddle in her love life. And why did she make Madison sound like a hermit? She spent tons of time around town working with patrons. Apparently, that didn't count to Ava. Not unless a man happened to be with her.

Madison forced a fake smile. "It's good to see you, too, Mrs. Gianini. How's the winery? Tessa said things are going well."

Ava waved off her comment. "They're fine. Aren't you going to introduce me to this handsome man you have here?"

She didn't *have* anyone. And Ava knew exactly who was with her.

"Of course, where are my manners?" Madison ground out. "This is Jake Colt. He's the new owner of Oak Hills. Jake, this is Ava Gianini, my best friend Tessa's mom."

"It's a pleasure to meet you, Mrs. Gianini." Jake stood and extended his hand to Ava.

"The pleasure is mine," Ava cooed, shaking his hand. "My, my, Madison you certainly have done well. Didn't I tell you he'd be perfect for you? I'm always right about these things, you know."

Except for the last dozen times, of course.

Madison could feel the blush burning up her cheeks. "I, uh…"

"Maybe you could give me some pointers. I seem to be failing miserably tonight," Jake joked.

If only he were failing instead of making her tingle all the way down to her toes.

Ava laughed. "I think you're the last person who needs any pointers. I bet you've never had a problem with women, not even a hiccup. But there's bound to be a first, and if anyone can give you a hard time, it's Madison. She's far too independent for her own good. She'll grow old with her camera if she's not careful. Which is where you come in to sweep her off her feet."

Madison wrenched her napkin into a tight twist under the table. "I'm right here, Mrs. Gianini."

"I'm just letting the man know a little bit about you."

"I appreciate the help, Mrs. Gianini, but I'd like to find out about Madison on my own. It's more fun that way. I'm glad I had the opportunity to meet you, though." Jake's gentle tone softened the firmness of his words, seamlessly giving Ava the boot while remaining polite.

Grateful and awed at his move, Madison fought to keep her jaw from dropping. Now, that was a knight in shining armor.

Ava's hand fluttered to her chest. "Oh my, you are a treat. Likewise. I look forward to seeing more of the two of you."

Ava excused herself to rejoin her friends. The instant she reached the table, the women leaned in, heavily engrossed in conversation, with someone poking her head up every few seconds to look back at Madison and Jake.

Madison fell back in her chair with a sigh of relief. "Thanks for getting rid of her. I can only stand so much of her at a time. I have no idea how Tessa and her sisters have survived for so many years."

"She's coming from a good place. She obviously cares for the people around her and wants to see them happy."

Madison blinked at him. She hadn't thought of Ava as anything but a nosy busybody with nothing to do but mess about in people's lives since her children had grown up. How had she missed for years what Jake was able to identify in a couple of minutes? And she thought she was the intuitive one.

What else had she misjudged about Jake? The question raised some challenging answers she didn't want to dwell on.

"Thank you for this evening and for your work on the contest," she said, scooting her chair back.

He stood up in an instant, helping her out of her seat and then picking up the rose, drying the stem, and handing it to her.

"Of course. I apologize if the meal was too … what was the phrase you used earlier? Hoity-toity?"

She winced, guilt creeping up on her as she accepted the flower. "I did say that, didn't I? Sorry, this isn't really what I'm used to."

He set his hand on the middle of her back, leaning close to her ear. "That's what I like best about you."

Her skin tingled under his touch and she swayed closer to him. Trouble. This was true, oh-so-tempting trouble.

"Why does the evening have to end here? Why don't we go dancing?" He guided her through the restaurant.

She noticed all the looks coming their way. What would people be saying in the morning about this?

She gave a nervous giggle. "Dancing? Are you serious? Where? The whole place shuts down around nine."

"I hate that about small towns. But I'm sure we have time for one dance."

"There are no clubs here."

"Who said anything about a club?"

Mischief colored his words, triggering a surge of curiosity and anticipation in her as he led her off the lobby to a dimly lit lounge with a pianist playing on a raised stage.

"We can't dance in the lounge," she said, taking in the few couples spread about the room, sipping drinks.

"Why not?"

"There's no dance floor and no one else is dancing."

"So? Who needs a dance floor? All I need is you." He tugged her into his arms and began swaying to the slow melody.

On instinct, she started to draw back, but then Ava's words came back to hit over the head like a sledgehammer. *She'll grow old with her camera if she's not careful.* Madison loved photography, but that sounded awful. A single dance couldn't hurt.

Her left hand dangled the rose behind his shoulder, her right hand tucked neatly into his. Her heart beat a rapid tune against her chest and straight to his as if no space existed between them. Their legs bumped against each other, each contact sending shockwaves through her bloodstream.

She heard murmurs around them and realized the spectacle they had created. Embarrassment flooded her senses. People would really be talking now. But then she looked up into Jake's smiling face and got caught in the sultry stare he sent her as everything else around them faded.

She nestled her forehead against his neck, taking in his crisp, fresh scent mixed with pure male.

His lips brushed against the top of her hair.

Her eyes drifted closed, then all too soon the song ended, bringing her back to her senses.

She pulled away. "I should get going."

For a moment, he seemed about to object, but then he took her hand and said, "I'll walk you out."

They strode out into the moonlight and up to her car.

He cupped her neck. "I hate to say goodnight."

She saw the craving in his azure eyes, felt it in the enticing pressure of his fingertips.

All of her senses purred in response, but she'd be down this road before. Believing in promises of forever, right up to the moment when Tucker had ditched her. She still remembered his stinging words and that fateful trip to Los Angeles.

The memory drenched her like a cold shower, and still it took every ounce of her restraint to move away from Jake. All the more reason she should back off.

"I'll say it then." She couldn't resist. She kissed his cheek. "Goodnight."

What was she doing?

She didn't wait for a response. She turned and slid into her car, pulling out into the brisk, dark night.

# CHAPTER EIGHT

The next morning, Madison ducked into Tea and Crumpets, a clattering of bells signifying her presence.

"Mrs. Jameson?" she called out.

"Back here, luv," Mrs. Jameson's heavy British accent came from the patio.

Madison made her way through the trinket-laden shop and empty restaurant to the bright outdoor sitting area with umbrella-shaded tables and a late summer garden bursting with an array of California fuchsia and goldenrod. The shop was open, but tea and scones wouldn't be served until the afternoon. A sweet scent still wafted in from the kitchen, though.

"Good morning," Madison greeted the older woman hunched over a large cardboard box.

"Good mornin'. I was just getting another box of teapots out." Mrs. Jameson struggled in her attempts to pick up the heavy box.

"Here, let me help you." Madison set her coffee aside and positioned herself on the other side of the box. "Ready?"

Mrs. Jameson nodded and together they lifted the container.

"It's goin' inside to the table on the right."

Madison backed her way through the open door to the table. They set the box down with a thud.

Mrs. Jameson rubbed her hands on the towel tucked into the waistband of her skirt. "Now, I assume you brought the photographs, dearie."

"Yes, I have them right here for you." Madison opened her satchel to remove a large envelope. "I think the ones of Gaarwine on the pony turned out the best."

If she had to take one more picture of a cute, pudgy-faced kid at their birthday, she would scream. Nothing wrong with the kids or the parties, and it gave her a great excuse to have delicious cake. But she wanted to cover bigger events than small birthdays.

Mrs. Jameson shuffled through the pictures. "These are lovely. Thank you."

"My pleasure."

Mrs. Jameson set the envelope down next to the box and put her arm around Madison's shoulders. "How's your mum? Are your parents holdin' up with the sale and all?"

Madison's heart plummeted. Didn't people have other things to talk about? "They're doing fine. Terrific, actually."

Mrs. Jameson gave her a squeeze. "Of course they are, they have that talented, gorgeous new bloke for a partner. I haven't seen him yet but from what I've heard, *I* wouldn't mind having him for a partner."

"I don't think Mr. Jameson would like that very much."

Mrs. Jameson moved to unload the box, stacking little teapots on the side. "Rubbish. He wouldn't be worried. He's secure in my affections, especially when it comes to a chap half my age. I'm not that kind of lady," she said, a spark in her eyes.

Madison laughed, some of her anxiety oozing away.

"But tell me, is he really as handsome as they say?"

"More so."

She couldn't very well lie.

Mrs. Jameson snapped her fingers. "I knew it. And I hear you've been spendin' a lot of time together. You can tell me, luv. Are you two datin'? How romantic after he saves your family's business." The older woman gave a deep sigh, fluttering her eyelashes.

Romantic? Saved? Not exactly. More like arrogantly commandeered, and Madison refused to even broach the word romantic.

"The whole town's talkin' about how we have another Eduardo and Aurelia story on our hands."

Goosebumps prickled her skin, her fingers squeezing the tiny teacup in a merciless grip. "Excuse me?"

"I mean we have another outsider stealing one of our girls. We're all wonderin' when Jake will swoop you off to New York."

Her hands trembled as she set down the china. Dread, hard and frigid, encapsulated her heart. Tucker had been an outsider and no one had associated them with the famed couple. But then, Tucker had promised they would make a life together here, not in a big city.

How could everyone compare her to Aurelia, who had abandoned her family in their time of need? She could never do such a thing. And what was all this talk about New York? But, of course, that's where Jake lived and his wife would live there, too.

He'd made it clear that small town life suited him about as well as a puffy, pink ball gown. No power on Earth, though, could get her to step foot in New York, leaving behind her family, this town, even with its overeager gossiping grapevine, and not to mention her business, her baby. Which left her biggest question, the one making sweat dampen the back of her neck: why did she care?

"Our relationship is strictly business, nothing personal, Mrs. Jameson," Madison said. Best to stick to her story and get out. "I have to go. I hope you enjoy the photos."

She snatched up her coffee.

"Of course, dearie. Cheerio. And bring that gorgeous gentleman back here with you, business or otherwise."

Mrs. Jameson waved at Madison as she dashed out the door.

She took in a refreshing gulp of air to steady herself. She couldn't remember the last time she had been the center of so much attention and she hated every minute of it. What would it be like to actually date Jake in the media storm that surrounded him?

The thought made her shudder, reminding her exactly why she had to guard herself against him. She needed an ally and she knew the perfect one—two as a matter of fact.

She cut through Serenity Square, city hall's bells jingling to signify the passing of the hour as she made her way to The Wine Cork. Pulling out her cell phone without breaking her stride, she warily avoided the fountain in the middle of the square, an exact replica of the one at Rancho de Serenidad with its massive stone cut into a sharp octagon and a thin pillar in the center with the Graciela family crest engraved on it, spurting out water. She and Aurelia? What were people thinking?

She didn't even wait for Tessa's greeting. "Are Jake and I the only thing this town is talking about? Tell me there's something more important going on to take up everyone's time."

"Sorry, but you guys are it. My mom won't stop chattering about it. She thinks you make a very cute couple."

Madison groaned. "This is terrible. No one can work with a member of the opposite sex around here without thinking they're involved."

"Not when that member looks like Jake."

"Thanks."

"I just wanted to be truthful. Should I meet you with chocolate?" Tessa asked.

"No. Well, maybe. I'll get back to you. I'm going to talk to Adam."

"I'm here if you need me. It's a pretty slow day."

Madison's heart warmed. "Thank you for being there for me."

"You're always there for me. It's a two-way street."

"Best street in town. I'll give you a call later." Madison hung up. She could feel her control over her emotions slipping. Never a good sign.

She reached the cool interior of The Wine Cork and went directly to the back room, finding Adam counting wine bottles.

He looked up from where he had been jotting down notes on his clipboard.

"Maddy, what's wrong?" he asked the instant he saw her face.

She threw her arms wide. "Everything."

A few of the workers cast her some odd glances.

"Right. Why don't we continue this in my office?"

He led her down the hall to a small room housing a dark wood desk and a few matching chairs.

"Sit." He indicated one of the seats. "Now, tell me what has you so worked up."

She sat down, clutching her satchel and coffee in her lap.

"I've had it up to here," she put her hand to her forehead, "with this town's busybody gossip. The only thing people speak to me about is Jake and the time I'm spending with him."

He rocked back in his chair. "I think it's you two dating that has people more caught up than the time you're spending together, as you put it. The only reason I haven't punched the guy's face in is because I can't believe you would ever really get involved with someone like him."

She saw the sliver of doubt in his eyes, undercutting the resolution in his voice.

An image of the rose Jake had given her last night that now sat in a vase on her nightstand flooded her thoughts, punctuated by the lingering feel of his arms encircling her as they danced together.

Her response came at a slightly higher pitch than she would have liked. "You're right. There's nothing going on between us besides some marketing."

As well as one kiss and some steamy daydreams on her part. But those were off limits.

"That's good, very good. How are the pictures coming along?"

She huffed out a breath. "The photos are turning out terrific. The hassle in getting them is another topic all together."

"What are you talking about?"

"Jake wants shots all over the area, highlighting what people can experience here, so he has all these excursions planned, but he won't tell me what they are so I can prepare. They're surprises."

"Must be going over great with you."

She grimaced. "Don't get me started."

"What have you guys done so far?"

"Just a hike, and I took some shots of the vineyard yesterday."

"You? On a hike? As much as I hate the man, I would have paid money to see that." He grinned.

She remembered her slip in the creek and Jake's subsequent rescue ... his hard muscles flinching under her fingernails, the strong feel of his arms holding her tightly, the steady beat of his heart.

She gripped her coffee cup as she downed the last of it.

"Any ideas what your next grand escapade is?"

"Actually, yes. It's later today so Jake thought it would be all right if I knew where we were going as long as he got to pick me up at my place."

"Your place?" The muscles in his shoulders tensed and a brusqueness invaded his tone.

"Yeah. We're going horseback riding."

He gazed at her in silence for several seconds before doubling over in laughter.

She threw the cup in the trash next to his desk with more force than necessary. "Go ahead, laugh it up."

He rubbed his eyes. "I'm sorry. I'm trying to picture my control freak sister on a large, semi-wild animal, and it's a hilarious scene in my mind."

"I don't find it so amusing."

"Then you need to find your sense of humor because it's missing."

She smiled at him, rising from her chair and adjusting her knee-length cream skirt and three-quarter sleeve matching jacket.

"I should get going," she said, making her way to the door.

"When and where is this once-in-a-lifetime event taking place?"

She paused with her hand on the doorknob, debating whether or not she should tell him. He was her brother, so what would be the harm? Then again, he was her brother and extremely protective of her, especially when it came to men.

"Two o' clock at Twin Oaks Farm. Why? Are you going to stop by?"

He fiddled with some papers on his desk. "Maybe, maybe not. But I should keep better tabs on this guy who's picking up my baby sister at her apartment all date-like. You going to try to stop me?"

"I know better and it's not a date."

She slipped out the door to the dark hallway, unease gripping her belly. She, Jake, and Adam in the same place at the same time was a powder keg waiting to explode.

•••

As Madison and Jake drove to the Twin Oaks Farm, Madison's anxiety over their upcoming ride grew with each passing second, so that by the time they reached their destination, her heart was pounding from fear and her palms were slick with sweat.

She didn't wait for Jake as she slid out of his Range Rover and nervously paced to where a few horses grazed near the white rail fence of a pasture.

He came up behind her.

Her nails bit into her hands. "Did I tell you how much I don't like outdoors stuff? That includes animals larger than myself."

Why would a person trust an animal with a crafty mind and so much physical power enough to sit on top of it with nothing but a saddle and a bridle?

He set his hands on her shoulders, giving them a reassuring squeeze. "Don't worry, I have it all taken care of."

She turned around to face him. "Really? How exactly?"

"You'll see."

He flicked a finger under her chin, the gesture at once disarming and comforting.

"Follow me." He took her hand and led her to a small office nearby.

If she had been in command of her emotions, she would have put a stop to his enticing, perilous contact. But, as so often was the case around him, she had lost all semblance of control.

He went in to make the arrangements for their ride while she waited outside, crossing and uncrossing her arms, checking her watch, fiddling with her sweater.

Finally, he emerged and led her to where a groom held a beautiful chestnut horse saddled and ready.

"Where's the other one?" she asked.

"What other one? We'll be taking one horse. Together."

She stood motionless.

The thought of being right up against him for the next couple of hours sent blood rushing to her head. It could only bring trouble. That worry, though, was vastly overshadowed by her apprehension about horseback riding, and knowing he would be guiding the horse instead of her eased her mind a great deal. The relief would be worth the price she paid.

He helped her onto the horse and then mounted behind her, nestling her close to him and taking the reins.

He steered the horse with an expert hand, leading them away from the stables at a gentle pace.

Her knuckles blanched as her fingers squeezed the front of the saddle.

"Just lean back and relax," he whispered in her ear.

She blew out a long breath, sinking back into the solid wall of his chest.

She felt his heat transfer through the thin barrier of clothes between them to warm her skin, soothing her frazzled nerves.

Closing her eyes, she took in the fresh scent of trees and flowers, listening to the rustle of leaves on the ground, the rhythmic thud of the horse's hooves. Her unease seeped away into the calm wind brushing against her face.

"I can't imagine Twin Oaks Farm usually allows guests to go on a ride without a guide, let alone two people on one horse," she said, taking in the open space of wild grass around them.

"I can very persuasive at times."

She pursed her lips. She knew the truth. "Your wallet can be."

He stiffened behind her and she understood she had crossed the line.

Being with Jake always unsettled her, ripping apart her prized composure and leaving her vulnerable. His statement, though, formed a firm reminder of all the reasons she should bury her inappropriate feelings for him. He might be talented, handsome, and charming, but he was also a rich, risk-taking playboy used to getting his way.

She straightened in an effort to put some space between them. "I'm sorry. I shouldn't have said that."

"I hope you realize money isn't always bad."

"Money isn't the issue; how a person gets it and uses it is."

"Investing my wealth in your parents' winery isn't a terrible thing."

She sighed. "No, but to my father it's like taking a handout. It's admitting he couldn't do it by himself."

"To your father, or to you?"

The truth of his accusation hit her square in the gut.

"You're right. I don't like accepting help from others, especially when it comes to my dream."

"Why?"

"I have to prove I can do it on my own, like my dad and my brother. They built their business from the ground up without assistance from other people, and I know I can do the same. Of course, in my father's case, you swooped in and took everything over in a minute after they spent years painstakingly developing it. You better be careful with my dad's dream."

"If the winery means so much to you, then why aren't you working there with your mom and dad?" he asked.

She bristled. "Because my parents taught me to have a vision and go after it with everything I have. My dream wasn't the winery, it's photography. But the winery is my dad's pride and joy. I refuse to let you or anyone else take it from him."

Her family loved the winery and she loved her family. The winery was still her home even if she didn't live there and it required the utmost protection.

His lips grazed her ear as he spoke in a low voice. "Madison, I want you to hear me loud and clear. I am not here to take anything from you. Understand me when I say I'm trying to help, not hurt your father. I know how important your family is to you. I'm asking you to trust me."

Trust him? His speech sounded great and even if she couldn't read his face, his tone signaled the honesty of his words. But trust him? She wasn't ready for that yet. Or for the hundreds of butterflies invading her belly at his sweet promise.

"What about your family? I know nothing about the real you," she asked.

He wavered for a split second. "My childhood was a lot different than yours. My father spent all of his time at the office. I didn't really see him much until I hit high school and, in his mind, became of age to learn the ropes at the company."

Her heart broke. "What about your mom?"

He tightened his grip on the reins. "She wasn't there."

"What do you mean? Where was she? Who raised you?"

"Nannies and boarding schools."

She didn't miss the fact that he had avoided her question about his mother.

"Here it is. This is the spot." He pulled the horse to a stop.

She looked around at the gnarled oak trees, sweeping grass, and open meadow with mint green hills in the background. The scene appeared pretty enough, but it was the same as what they had been passing for a half hour now. She had a feeling his choice had more to do with putting an end to their conversation than his real plan for pictures.

He swung out of the saddle in one fluid movement.

"Need a hand?" He touched her ankle, giving it a soft squeeze.

She recalled her slip on the hike. She had to make up for it. She could do this by herself.

"I'm fine. Thanks."

She swung her leg over the back end of the horse and almost made it to the ground until her other foot caught in the stirrup. Yanking her foot out, she lost her balance and went tumbling down, landing with a thud on Jake.

Their legs intertwined, dust covered every inch of them, her breathing became heavy, and her face rested inches above his own.

His cool blue eyes took her in as his hands gripped her. "Yeah, you're fine."

Her pulse raced as she struggled to her feet, searching desperately around her. "My camera. Where is it? Is it okay?"

He rose, swatting dirt from his jeans. "The shoulder strap got caught on the horn of the saddle. It's over there."

She grabbed the dangling satchel holding her camera, clutching the precious bag to her chest.

"Thank goodness," she rasped.

"I'm okay, too, by the way."

She swiveled around. "I'm sorry I landed on you."

He strode up to her, toying with a few loose strands of her hair.

"Tell you what, you can land me on me any day as long as I can pass up your camera on your list of priorities."

Little did he know how fast he was zooming up that list.

Before she knew it, he had unhooked the clasps on her bag and had a hand on her camera.

"What are you doing?"

She tried to seize his arm, but he slipped out of her grasp and held up the camera as his trophy.

"A little payback."

He snapped off shots of her from different angles, not even bothering to look through the lens or line anything up.

"Give it back."

She ran to him, jumping up to reach the camera, but he lifted it up out of her reach.

His laughter only deepened her annoyance. She didn't like being on the other end of a shot.

His arm caught hold of her and her hands slammed against his chest. Her frustration trickled away, replaced by a far different sensation.

"All you ever have to do is say please."

"Please," she whispered.

He lowered the camera to her. His thumb stroked the middle of her back.

She pulled away, putting a few paces between them. "I should get started."

She lined up the first picture, trying to make sense of what had happened. Twice now he had caught her. She had to admit he made her feel safe despite the excursions they went on and the fact he was supposed to be her enemy.

He had the unique ability of sending her off in two different directions at the same time. Hot and cold. Fire and Ice. Reactions as opposite as they themselves were. In the end, though, only one could win.

• • •

Horseback riding yesterday had gone better than Jake had hoped, and by the end Madison seemed to loosen up more about their "adventures." Tonight's dinner at the Carmichaels', though, was a different story. The feast spread before them, intermingled with candles, appeared so serene, with its delicious smells of rosemary and lemon. If only the people around it were just as peaceful, he'd be able to enjoy it. From the moment he'd walked in the door, Adam had given him the cold shoulder and when Adam deigned to speak to him his words were curt and just this side of confrontational.

He should have anticipated as much with everyone buzzing about him and Madison, especially after their late afternoon ride.

"Tell me straight out, Jake. What are your intentions with my sister?" Adam laid into him before the bread could even be passed around.

Rose sputtered her wine, recovering behind her napkin, while Thomas tensed his shoulders.

Jake kept his attention on Adam, but caught a glimpse of Madison's pale face from the corner of his eye. "I think it's rude to discuss someone in the third person when they're sitting at this very table."

"Stop with the bull."

"Adam," Rose warned, giving a sign to Thomas to step in.

Jake studied Madison's countenance. He witnessed the debate, not knowing whether to support her brother or him, raging within her.

"All right. I think Madison is incredibly talented. Her pictures have been phenomenal, and I have high hopes for the success of this new promotional sweepstakes."

Adam slammed his hand on the arm of the chair, shooting to his feet. "And stop with the marketing smokescreen. I will not let you turn my sister into another one of your casual affairs."

Jake shoved his chair back, his fists grinding into the table as he bent toward Adam.

"Enough! Both of you." Madison stood up. "Adam, how dare you?"

"I'm looking out for you. What's he doing?"

"Neither one of you is being anything but selfish and prideful," she fumed.

"Everyone sit down," Thomas commanded. "I will not have an argument at my dinner table. Is that understood?"

Thomas looked between Jake and Adam for confirmation.

Madison took her seat first.

Adam nodded, sitting down, and Jake followed suit, keeping a watchful glare on Adam, who returned in kind with a hard scowl of his own.

Thomas grabbed his wine glass. "Good. Now that's settled, we can move on to a more pressing topic. It'll be harvest time soon and we need a game plan to maximize our exposure this year during the wine club member dinner as well as the festival wine tastings."

"I'll be busy with the restaurant. It's a hectic time for us, too, with the festival, but let me know whatever you need done and I'll be there," Adam said.

"Thank you. Jake, what about you? Do you have any ideas for this year?" Adam opened his mouth to interrupt, no doubt with a critical remark, but suddenly winced in pain, shooting daggers at Madison.

The weight that had been pressing on Jake throughout the meal lifted. His spitfire remained on his side. At least for now and that's all that mattered.

Jake set his fork down. "A few, actually. Rose and I are working on taking the wine club member dinner up a notch this year. The picnic tables I ordered for the new outdoor seating area should be here in time for the special wine tastings during the festival. I plan on having a selection of salami and cheese available during the tastings as well. And, of course, we'll offer specials on certain vintages."

"Is that all that *we'll* be doing? I'm so glad you saved my dad the trouble of messing with all that nasty stuff like giving input on his own winery. It's much easier with a dictator around." Madison threw her napkin on the table, crossing her arms in front of her.

He'd offended her. He hadn't meant to, but he was accustomed to being in charge. Asking for advice, or worse, permission, was not his strong suit.

"Easy, Madison," Thomas said. "Jake's suggestions are sound, and I have no problem implementing all of them. You'll still be here to help us through harvest and all the celebrations, right?"

"Of course," Jake answered without missing a beat.

The skeptical expression Madison sent him cut him to the core and worried him far more than the fury emanating off of Adam.

"What's next for your marketing adventures, Jake?" Rose asked, shifting in her seat, obviously uncomfortable with the hostility surrounding her.

"That's a surprise, but I will say it has something to do with water."

"I don't like water," Madison responded in a flat tone.

"Like you don't flying?"

"Just like that."

"You want to back out?" Jake's heart thumped against his chest as he waited for her answer.

In the stillness, every stare fixed upon her.

She didn't even bat an eyelash.

"No. I'll do it."

"Bad decision," Adam grumbled.

Jake barely heard him over the relief pouring over him. He hadn't realized how vital her partnership in all of this had become, how essential spending time with her was to him, and how endangered their arrangement could get if he didn't fight for it.

# CHAPTER NINE

Madison stared at herself in the mirror above her dresser, tying the strings of her emerald bikini behind her back. She had two outfits on her bed currently under debate. It would have been easier to pick something if she knew where Jake planned to take her this afternoon, but all she knew was to prepare for water.

Unlike flying, she didn't fear water. She had a great dislike of its uncontainable aspects, though, and so had never bothered to become familiar with it or spend much time near it.

She wavered between her two clothing options. One would keep her warmer, but the other would repel water better. Would they get wet? Or would they stay on the shore? And what about the man behind all these excursions? She hated to admit it, but Jake had earned some of her trust. All of their photo ops had gone well, minus a little tumble at the waterfall, and would highlight the area and vineyard well. Still, how would he react after last night's heated debate at the dinner table? Her dad had assured her he agreed with all of Jake's "suggestions" for the winery. His word, not hers. She took Jake's statements at face value, and they didn't fall into the advice category. They sat firmly under commands.

And yet, the instant her doorbell rang, her nerves tingled all the way down her spine and a tickling sensation teased her belly.

She snatched the pair of pants closest to her, which happened to be white capris, and walked out of the room carrying her tank top and jacket with her.

A knock sounded through her apartment.

"Just a minute," she called, struggling to pull her shirt on as she strode through the living room.

She huffed in defeat, tossing it on the couch to throw open the door.

Jake's appreciation and desire were evident in his slow, methodical stare.

"Wow. If I had known you were going to wear that, I would have set up the aquatic part of our promotional plan a long time ago."

She laughed, motioning him inside. "Wait until you suffer through all of the harassment you're going to receive for dragging me into the water."

"It's worth it, trust me."

"We'll see if you keep thinking that. So, we are going in the water, not just near it?" Her small victory would have been complete if not for the churning in her stomach at the idea of being submerged.

He grinned. "Something like that."

"This mystery thing is overrated." She huffed. "I just need to get my camera and I'm ready."

She tugged her top on, slipped into her jacket, and grabbed her camera bag.

"After you," she said, following him down to his Range Rover.

She studied his profile from the passenger seat and saw none of the nervous energy coursing through her in him. He appeared so calm and collected. It irritated her. What game was he playing?

He made a turn out of town. "I have a quick stop to make. I need to pick up something. It won't take long."

"Yeah. Sure. Okay."

At least he didn't grill her about yesterday evening's dinner catastrophe. But with Adam's accusations, the town's gossip, and her own mixed feelings, she had to get a better grasp of things.

"What's the deal with us?" She blurted out the first words that came to her.

He shrugged. "It's no secret I'm interested in you. I've been pretty up front about it."

"You've been interested in lots of women."

"That's true, but it doesn't change one iota of what I feel for you."

"For right now."

This time, he cringed. "Sweetheart, no one can see the future."

She bristled even though she couldn't deny the truth of his words.

"Let's just have some fun with this chemistry between us," he added.

How romantic. At least he was honest. Tucker never had been. She dug her nails into the seat leather.

"I don't date for fun. I date someone to discover if there's any prospect for a long-term, serious relationship with them. I will not let myself become one of the many girls featured with you on the tabloid covers."

He sighed. "I'm not a fan of the press. They do a poor job of presenting the real situation, and I wouldn't want you involved in something like that, either. But, I'm not a serious relationship kind of guy."

"Oh, I know. You live in the moment and don't look beyond it."

"Maybe you should try it. It's better than not living at all and letting the moment pass you by."

She slumped back. His speech hit her heart hard. She couldn't imagine having a fling with him. She never had flings. On the other hand, she had an inkling she would regret it if she didn't pursue her feelings for him.

All her considerations ceased, though, when she saw the welcome sign for the airport. All her senses went on high alert.

She could make do with water, but she drew a firm line when it came to flying. No way, no how would she go up in the air.

"What are you doing? Why are we here? Are you crazy?"

He entwined his fingers with hers. "Calm down. I'm not taking you flying. At least not today. I need to pick up something I left in my MD 600N."

"I assume that's your helicopter?"

"Yes."

Her unease leaked away a little, but she remained cautious as he parked the car and led her to the helicopter that had landed smack dab in the middle of her life. The smell of oil and burnt rubber filled her nose.

He offered her his hand. "Come on, see the inside."

She hesitated, hovering outside the open doors.

"It's on the ground and it's not going anywhere," he reminded her.

"All right."

He hoisted himself in first before turning and helping her into one of the cream leather seats.

She had expected a tub of nuts and bolts with blades on the top. The reality, though, struck her. There was a back row of seats in the same supple white as the front. Three windows on each side as well as large front windows allowed ample amounts of bright sun into an interior that was small, but roomier than she had envisioned. Before her, a slew of confusing controls and dials littered the dashboard.

"How do you keep track of all of this stuff?" she asked, pointing to the control panel.

"It's fairly simple once you get the hang of it. Those are the collective and cyclic control sticks." He indicated each one in turn. "What do you think?"

"It's nice for a flying contraption of torture."

He flicked a finger under her chin. "I'll get you up in the air yet."

"Not gonna happen, Colt. You should stop while you're ahead."

"We'll see." He picked up a set of keys from a compartment and tucked them into the pocket of his board shorts. "Ready?"

"To get out of here? Not a minute too soon."

She climbed down, making a beeline for the car as soon as her feet hit the ground.

He followed her at a slower pace after locking up everything.

She clicked her seatbelt in place. "So, where are we going?"

He grinned. "And ruin the surprise? Not a chance."

"I give up. Just drive."

"Yes, ma'am." He slipped on a pair of aviator sunglasses.

She stewed in her seat, staring out the window. Before too long, they got on the freeway, and soon the rolling hills, dotted with oak trees, seemed to be speeding past them.

It took about twenty minutes to reach their destination and her stomach hit the floor at the sight before her. He parked the car in front of a secluded beach spot vacant of any other signs of life.

The ocean? She had anticipated a lake, secretly hoped for a pool. Never had she believed he would bring her here. The sea was the most untamed part of nature and he wanted to take her out in it?

She got out of the SUV, slamming the door behind her, not from anger—there wasn't any space for that with all the anxiety permeating through her—but from sheer horror.

She noticed two kayaks set up and ready to go near a moss-covered cliff face. He must have prearranged for them to be here. Was there no end to what his money could buy?

It couldn't buy her, and she should well remember the canyon of differences between his world and hers.

She shook her head. "Uh-uh. Sorry. I'm not facing the wild sea in some rickety canoe."

"They're sturdy kayaks and everything is going to be fine."

"Did I tell you I'm not the best swimmer?"

He rubbed his hands up and down her arms, warming every inch of her.

"We have life vests if you want." He held up a bulky yellow vest.

"How am I supposed to move around in that thing to get the shots we'll need?" She poked the sand with the tip of her sandal. "Do you think I'll need it?"

"No. This is a calm inlet. There aren't many waves, and I'll be right there with you. I won't let anything happen to you. Trust me."

Could she? He'd asked her to do that before and she'd resisted. What about now?

"Okay. Keep the trip short, though."

"Thank you."

He placed the life vests against some rocks and returned to the Range Rover, digging around for something in the back.

"You'll need these," he said, presenting her with a watertight bag and waterproof case.

She studied both items. She didn't have much use for them since she never spent time near water, especially not with her prized Canon, but she knew they were top of the line and very expensive.

"I can't accept these. They're way too much."

"I know how important your camera is to you. What else are you going to do with it out on the ocean?"

He had a point. She had to protect her camera—she couldn't afford to replace it—and she couldn't be a photographer without one.

She took the case and the bag. "Good point. But I'm returning them to you after this ludicrous photo session is over."

"Fine, if that's the only way I can get you to take them."

He finished getting things packed up in the kayaks while she adjusted her long-range lens and stowed her camera snugly in the gear he had given her before strapping it into her kayak.

The kayaks rested near the water's edge, ready to be pushed in. Madison clenched and unclenched her slick hands, pure panic pulsing within her.

"I thought you were the big, tough girl ready to send my butt back to New York. Are you coming or are you going to whimper on the shore?"

That did it. She couldn't back down now. Not to her rich, conceited enemy who had stolen her family's winery and was getting frighteningly close to stealing her heart as well.

"You're going to eat your words, Colt." She pushed the kayak into the lapping waves.

"I hope so, sweetheart." He went in behind her with the other boat.

He steadied hers with one hand while keeping a hold on his with the other so she could clamber in.

"You ready?"

Unease slithered up her spine. "Yes."

She fiddled with the paddle, trying to figure out how to use the darn thing.

"Put the paddle into the water with a firm stroke, then switch to the other side with another stroke. You'll get a rhythm going soon." He demonstrated the right way to handle the kayak with the same proficiency he showed in everything he attempted.

She struggled to get the strokes right but managed enough to keep up with him. His pace slowed to match her own, and she wondered how fast he would be going if not for her.

Once she got the hang of paddling, she began to notice the serene peace and beauty surrounding her. The shimmering blue of the water, the gentle breeze whispering around her, the caw of seagulls circling overhead. She watched in amazement as a pelican dove underwater after a fish.

But what heightened her enjoyment of this adventure, what made her feel safe enough to relax into it, was the man kayaking next to her. She had no doubt he could and would guard her, a belief that freed her to explore all sorts of crazy, taboo possibilities, like taking him up on his offer to see where their mutual attraction took them.

"This is incredible. I have to get a picture." She got hold of her camera, no easy feat considering all the protection surrounding it and having to fight to keep her paddle from falling into the water, and set up a shot of a seal swimming off to her right.

"Does that mean you're happy you came out with me?" He looked every bit the cocky male with his little smirk and confident stroke.

"As much as it pains me to admit it, yes. This is breathtaking and the shots will be perfect for the sweepstakes. Who wouldn't want to win a trip here?"

He chuckled. "I'm glad you approve."

She zoomed in on a pelican. "Why don't you like to talk about your dad?"

She didn't want to fall for a man she knew so little about, after all.

"He's a sore subject."

"Well since you dragged me kicking and screaming all the way out here, indulge me." She stowed her camera to better focus on him and took up her paddle again.

"When you put it that way, how can I refuse? What do you want to know?"

"What's your relationship with him like?"

He kept his gaze on the horizon. "Cold to say the least. He doesn't see me as anything more than an heir to his company and I've never forgiven him for not being a father to me." He shook his head, disgust contorting his features. "Life is one big business deal to him. Our relationship is built on negotiations." The muscles in his shoulders bunched under his shirt and his pace quickened, each stroke more powerful and determined than the last, as if he could outrun the bad thoughts their conservation triggered.

He regained his composure and reduced his speed, waiting for her to catch up.

The waves picked up a little at this distance from shore, but she finally had a steady stride going.

"Is that why you travel so much? To get away from him?"

"Bingo. It's why I do most of what I do. It's hard to think about Clayton when I'm hanging on the side of a mountain or out on the open sea."

She had to agree that nothing seemed to touch you out here. For instance, her concerns about finances and her parents hadn't reached her. Maybe that's why hope sprouted in her. "You could just pick a place to live, far away from him."

"I'd get bored and move on to the next location. I haven't found a reason to stay somewhere."

Could she ever be reason enough?

"Have you ever considered taking the time to figure out what you're really passionate about?"

He stared her straight in the eye. "Not until recently."

She felt like she did when she had the perfect shot set up in her lens: giddy, with the world at her fingertips.

"Look. Don't miss it." He pointed off to the left where a dolphin leapt out of the ocean in a graceful arch.

She rushed to get a picture, not wanting to miss the great photo op. She snapped away at the pod of dolphins playing together.

Once the animals moved on, she packed her camera away. She had to admit this was fun.

She tilted her face up to the sun, reveling in the adrenaline rush of being out on the sea, taking part in the splendor around her.

When she looked down, a single dolphin gracefully skimmed the surface in a perfect arch, close enough she was sure she could touch it. She reached out, leaning ever farther over the side of the kayak, her fingers almost brushing the gray skin.

"Madison, no!" Jake shouted, the instant before she capsized into the cool water below.

• • •

The instant Madison disappeared beneath the waves, Jake dove in after her, gut-wrenching fear fueling his every kick. He spotted her a little ways under the overturned kayak, moving her arms one above the other in an attempt to reach the surface. He grabbed hold of her and swam up to the light, both breaking the surface at the same time and gulping in air.

"Are you all right?" he asked, checking her face, her arms, and any part of her body within reach, desperate to be certain she had no injuries.

"I'm okay," she sputtered. "You came after me pretty fast. I'm not that bad of a swimmer."

He grinned, keeping a firm grip on her. That was his spitfire, all spunk and bravado even with a face as white as fresh fallen snow on the Alps.

"I didn't want to take any chances. I did promise I wouldn't let anything happen to you."

"Your promises are that good, huh?"

He swept a drenched strand of hair off her face. "Yes, especially when it comes to you."

He could have been too late. He could have lost her, and still he wanted to make her more promises. That wasn't a Jake Colt he even recognized.

"Let's get you back in. I'll help you into my kayak and then we can turn yours over so I can take it back to shore." He guided her alongside his kayak, steadying it while still holding on to her. "Can you hoist yourself up?"

"As long as I do better than dismounting from the horse."

She pulled herself up and he helped push her into the seat.

"Are you settled?"

"Just peachy." She hugged herself tight, shivering.

"We'll get to shore and get you warm. It won't take long." He pulled over the overturned kayak.

"My camera," she shrieked as if just remembering it now that she was out of the sea.

"You stowed it before you tipped over, so I'm sure it's fine. We have to get the water out of the kayak before we can turn it over. Take the front end and heave it up over your lap. I'll push and guide it from my end."

She bit her lower lip but did as he instructed.

"Now we're going to rock it back and forth to empty it. Ready?"

"I understand."

Water poured out of the kayak, dissipating into sprinkles of droplets.

"We're going to flip it over to my right."

They turned the kayak back over, joy lighting her eyes at the sight of the waterproof bag still strapped in, safe and snug.

"Thank goodness it's all right. These excursions of yours are way too risky for my equipment. I'm glad you brought the bag and case. You saved me and my camera."

While she kept the kayak stable, he lifted himself into it and then yanked the paddle leash to grasp the paddle, securing it in front of him, before taking hold of another line to attach to her kayak. He didn't think she was up for paddling back on her own so he planned to tow her.

He worked on the knot at the bow. "I think you're more concerned about the welfare of your camera than you are about your own self on our adventures."

She bent her head, murmuring, "It's just so expensive."

"But you're priceless."

She looked up and he caught her gaze. He saw the same mixture of passion and bewilderment there that hummed through his entire body.

"I'm going to tow you back, but if you can paddle some we'll reach the shore faster."

"Of course." She seized her paddle.

Good thing he had requested leashes for the paddles to fasten them to the kayaks.

He used all his strength to propel them forward as fast as he could manage. She must be freezing and he had to get her to shore. Sweat beaded down his back from the exertion, but all he could think about was the second she'd hit the water.

He hadn't been so terrified of losing something since he'd been ten years old—an unsettling thought for someone with no real attachments to anyone or anything.

When they reached the shore, he hopped out to assist her and haul the kayaks up onto the sand.

He enfolded her in his arms, settling her against his chest for heat and stroking her soaked hair. "We have to get you out of these wet clothes."

She started to protest but gave up. "Warmth would be good, but no peeking, Colt. I mean it."

He winked. "Never."

He headed to the SUV for the spare clothes he had brought with him.

"I think I'll keep the waterproof bag and case after all as payment for almost wrecking my camera, not to mention me in the process."

Remorse assailed him. He had pushed her to go out on the water with him, had recommended she not wear a life vest. She had appeared to enjoy kayaking, though, until she'd tipped over.

She probably hated it now. She was still shaking from the cold.

He wanted to help her shed her fears and experience life, not just live it. Her leaving her comfort zone and taking a chance was one of the sexiest attributes about her and the one he relished the most. Was he really the right person, though, to teach her about life when he was only living half of one himself with no relationships, familial or otherwise, to speak of?

He found his extra set of board shorts, shirt, and jacket and walked back to her. "I'm sorry about what happened." He held out the clothes along with a towel for her.

She eyed them warily. "Are you serious?"

"It's either these or the towel."

She snatched the ball of clothes out of his hands in a flash.

He chuckled. "Shoot. I was hoping for the towel."

"Not today."

"Next time." He set the towel on the hood of the Range Rover for her. "I'll give you some privacy."

He went over to check the kayaks.

A half hour later, with everything packed up, he secured Madison in the passenger seat and cranked on the car heater to ward against the dipping temperature of the setting sun.

"Better?"

"Hmm, much." She leaned her head back, her eyelids drooping down.

Backing out of the small lot, he studied her profile.

He liked taking care of her. He could get used to this arrangement.

# CHAPTER TEN

Madison curled into the passenger seat of Jake's Range Rover, the gentle rhythm of the car driving down the freeway lulling her. She never slept well in vehicles, but she did next to him. He kept wearing her out.

His fresh, masculine cologne clung to his clothes, enveloping her in their rugged scent. She breathed it in deep, relishing the feeling of attachment to him it gave her.

She had never been so petrified as when her body had struck the water, but then he had rushed in after her, so powerful and strong as he lifted her to the surface and settled her in the kayak. Best not to imagine what would have happened if he hadn't been there to save her. Of course, she wouldn't have been in such a mess if not for him.

Despite capsizing into the ocean, though, she liked being out there with him, right in the middle of nature, just as she had enjoyed horseback riding and hiking. She hadn't been in command on any of their adventures, but she relished each memory. His presence was the key ingredient to her happiness. Her emotions for Jake had spiraled out of control. She was at a crossroads and had a decision to make: move forward or throw it all into reverse.

The car stopped, jarring her from thoughts. They'd arrived back at her place.

Jake turned to her. "How about a shower and I'll make us dinner?"

"You cook?" She could feel her eyes open wide like globes.

"Don't look so shocked."

"I thought all of your meals consisted of restaurants. The high-end variety."

"Many do, but when I have the opportunity I like to make some myself."

She opened the car door. "This I have to see."

"There's no watching from the sidelines—you'll be helping me."

She flat out laughed as they made their way into her apartment. "I'm not surprised. You've been ruling over me since you got here, telling me what to do and when to do it."

"I'm not the controlling one. That's my father's department. Trust me, my way is better, and if you saw Clayton you'd agree with me."

"How can you say you're not controlling? You've been managing me nonstop."

"No, I'm not managing you. I'm trying to get you to let loose a little. To see what happens when you don't have every aspect of your life all planned out and tidy." He brushed his fingers across her cheek. "I want to see you *lose* control."

Her thoughts became fuzzy and she fumbled for something to say. "I'm going to wash Mother Nature out of my hair. The kitchen is around the corner. Make yourself comfortable and good luck finding anything in my fridge besides frozen dinners."

"I'm sure it's not that bad."

She walked down the hallway to her bedroom. "Give me a minute and I'll give you your clothes back."

Closing the door, she stripped off Jake's clothes and slipped on a robe. When she stepped out again, she ran right into his rock solid chest.

"Sorry." He grabbed her shoulders, steadying her.

She cleared her throat. "That's okay. Here are your clothes."

He accepted the rumpled pile. "Your fridge is appalling."

"I warned you."

"I'm going to head to the store really quick while you shower."

"Oh. Thanks. And thanks for rescuing me."

"Anytime." He stepped closer. "Will you be okay?"

"Yes."

"Because I could stay. We could shower together. Save some water."

She giggled. "Get out, Colt."

He beamed, striding back out to the living room.

Crossing over to her bathroom, she started the shower. She saw now the smart, capable, kind Jake behind the rich-boy façade.

Could she trust her judgment, though? Tucker had said he'd left the fast paced, corporate life behind him, but in the end he'd been biding his time and she'd been a passing amusement.

She stepped under the spray. Heat seeped through her skin to warm every part of her, the shock of capsizing circling down the drain with the shampoo.

In its place, a niggling memory toyed with her, about Jake's suggestion earlier regarding playing things out between them, having fun. The concept seemed so foreign to her, yet so tempting, like the man making the offer.

Perhaps he had a point and she hadn't been taking full advantage of life. She had conquered the challenges he threw in front of her, and gained new confidence in exploring uncharted territory. And if there was ever uncharted territory for her, it was having a fling—no commitments, no promises.

She had never met a man who infuriated and thrilled her like Jake. She always went out with men who played it safe and stayed close to home, with the exception of Tucker, who'd lied about everything. But the one who got her pulse racing, who revealed to her a new side of herself she hadn't known existed, was Jake Colt. He was nothing she had expected and everything she wanted.

She had gone the serious relationship route in the past. She had tried—oh how she had tried—both before and after Tucker. And nothing had panned out. On the contrary, she'd been humiliated. Tucker had been filled with assurances of forever and, in the end, used her as a temporary stopover on his way to the big leagues, as he called them. Jake made it clear from the beginning that Serenity Creek couldn't be farther from the place he called home and long term didn't exist in his vocabulary. At least this time, she knew the risks up front.

Some casual dating might be the change she needed. Could she do it? Could she let go and cut loose with Jake? See where their attraction took them, knowing full well he might get bored with Serenity Creek and leave at any minute?

She smiled. Exploring the fire kindling between them would be worth getting a little singed.

● ● ●

Jake poured two glasses of wine, positioning one on the counter for Madison before unloading the grocery bag and organizing the mixings for a salad along with the fresh garlic, shallots, and chicken, for coq au vin.

He took a sip of the pinot noir and found it exceptional, even though he usually preferred cabernet sauvignons. Somehow, he had developed a softer taste for Oak Hill's vintages, much like he had for the owner's daughter.

He glanced around Madison's residence, the size of which equaled many of the suites he had stayed in, taking in the details. Pictures of family and friends filled the walls and tables. The worn couches were accented with hand-knit blankets. Instead of feeling disconnected from it all, he felt grounded, and it all had to do with the woman showering in the other room.

He liked the new sensation, the idea of roots and planting some of his own with her … of taking an honest look at what a serious relationship could bring and the possibilities it held.

He had dangled off the side of steep mountains hundreds of feet above the ground, but the thought of settling down scared him as nothing had before. Especially settling down in a small town like Serenity Creek. Still, it gave him a greater rush of adrenaline and excitement than any climb in the world.

He gripped the edge of the counter, gulping down the wine as he heard footsteps coming down the short hallway.

"Better?" he asked.

"Much."

"For you." He handed her a glass of wine.

Sampling the wine, she said, "Mmmm. Delightful. Nice choice." She strode up behind him, placing her hand on his shoulder. "What do we have going on here?"

"Coq au vin."

"You actually make it?"

He chuckled. "Yes, and you're going to as well."

"You have high hopes for my cooking talents."

"I have great faith in you." He slipped his arm around her.

They chopped, sliced, and laughed their way through making the salad and getting the chicken ready to simmer on the stove.

"The coq au vin has to cook for about thirty minutes." He started the timer on his phone.

"We can relax in the living room for a little while."

She led the way, turning on her miniscule electric fireplace and pouring them each another serving of wine.

"It's odd to have such cool nights even in the summer." He took a seat next to her on the couch.

She shrugged. "It's almost fall. That's why grapes do so well here: warm days and chilly nights."

"So your dad told me." He raised his glass. "To Oak Hills and the family behind it. Cheers."

"Cheers." She clinked her glass against his, the hum reverberating around them.

"You have a nice apartment."

"It's nothing compared to what you're used to, I'm sure." She shot him a skeptical look.

He grinned. "That might be why I like it."

"What about you? Where's your home?" She curled her feet under her.

"Nowhere."

"You have to live somewhere."

"I have a penthouse in New York and a flat in London, but neither place is home. They're just spaces to store some of my things. I travel all the time and I'm never in one area for very long."

How much longer would he be here, facing his past everyday? Leaving had been all he'd wanted since he'd arrived, but now everything had become more complicated, twisted together with Madison.

"What about your family? Where do you guys go for the holidays?"

"We don't. I spend that time by myself in the Alps, skiing." He gazed at his feet.

She grabbed his hand. "I'm sorry."

He kissed it. "It's nothing."

The warmth of her touch, though, meant everything, banishing the ugliness of his thoughts.

"Why do you work for your father when it's obvious you don't like it?"

"I don't work for him."

She raised her eyebrows, confusion marring her face.

"I work for Colt Enterprises, not him. And I don't do much of that either."

"Why not?" she asked.

"You're full of questions tonight."

She sipped her wine. "It's the price you pay for our kayaking experience."

"Pretty steep, but when you put it that way." He crossed his long legs at the ankles.

"So?" she encouraged. "Why don't you work?"

"I haven't found anything that really interests me in the company. Clayton would love nothing more than to see me spend every waking hour, which to him is every hour, wheeling and dealing for the company and obeying his every word. Colt Enterprises is everything to him, and he needs someone to keep things going the way he wants when he's gone. Instead, he got me."

"Why not quit, then? Are you interested at all in the business?"

He scratched the back of his head. "My great-grandfather launched it. As much as I don't get along with my father, he's the only family I have and the corporation is part of that. Besides, I could run Colt Enterprises on my own terms if I stick around."

"Is that what you want?"

"I have no idea what I want."

She spread her hand on her chest. "I'm shocked. I thought you had everything you wanted."

He sat forward, curling a strand of her hair around his finger. He gave it a tender tug. "Not yet."

The longing in her eyes mirrored his own.

She licked her lips. "So you do have some idea of what you would like."

"I know what I desire in this moment and it's right in front of me."

The electric current buzzing between them shot straight to his heart.

"What about in the next moment and the one after that? What do you aim for outside of the here and now?" She tucked her hair behind her ear.

"Why is that so important to you?" He sank back in the couch, deflated. It always came down to long-term plans with her, and there she had him at a complete loss.

"Everyone has a dream. Everyone has plans for the future. Maybe you've never had to because everything's been given to you."

"Anything I've ever received has had strings attached to it."

"Exactly. You've been told what to do and when to do it. You've never had a chance to discover what you want most in your own life."

He watched her in absolute silence, shock rolling through him. No one had ever understood that aspect of himself or taken the time to care. "You're right. Maybe this is my chance to find out. So, does this mean I've been taken off your adversary hit list?"

She cocked her head to the side. "Maybe."

"Progress at last." His phone buzzed. "The coq au vin should be ready."

"Good, because the aroma is making my stomach grumble. I don't think anything so elaborate has ever come out of my kitchen before."

He helped her up. "Hopefully, it won't be the last."

"We'll see. Depends on how good it is," she teased.

He winked. "I'm not worried, then."

They arranged everything, complete with a single pillar candle on Madison's kitchen table, big enough to accommodate two chairs and nothing more.

She sampled the chicken, sighing with obvious delight. "Wow. This is amazing."

"Thank you. It helps to have a first-rate sous chef."

"Me? I chopped stuff and followed orders, nothing more. But it was a lot of fun."

"How is it your mother is such a phenomenal cook, you assist her on Friday nights, and you still don't like to cook?"

"I don't help her every Friday, only the ones where I don't have pictures to edit or a shoot to wrap up before dinner. Work is more important to me than what I eat, and warming something up takes a lot less time than actually making it."

Concern trickled down his back. "I'm beginning to understand why you value your camera so much. Is there anything in your life that takes a higher priority than your job?"

"It's not a job, it's my dream, and of course there are more significant things in my life." She squared her shoulders.

"Name one."

"My family."

"What else?"

She shut her mouth, glaring at him. "There's nothing wrong with giving my work such a vital position in my life. Building something from the ground up takes effort and a lot of it."

His worry grew. Would she ever put him above her photography? He could facilitate her dream if she would only let him.

"It goes faster with assistance from another person."

"I can stand on my own two feet."

"So you've told me. Your brother has a different opinion, I take it."

"You're talking about last night's dinner?"

He tightened his grip on his knife. "He takes protection to a whole new level. Not that I blame him when it comes to you. You don't seem to appreciate it, though."

"For the same reason I don't want help with my business, I don't need it. I can take care of myself."

"And that's why you're taking pictures for me in exchange for a paycheck because you don't need me." He massacred his chicken.

She dropped her fork with a sharp clang. "No, that's not it. We have a contract. I'm not taking a hand out."

"I didn't say you were and that's not what I intended."

"What did you intend? When you began this whole thing with marketing pictures and the sweepstakes, what was your plan?"

He could lie. The truth might not put him in the right light, but he had made a choice at the start of this game and he had to own up to it.

"To get close to you. I figured you wouldn't turn down the job offer, especially with your parents' winery on the line."

She sat silent for a while before saying, "So Adam was right. You really were doing all of this to date me, not for Colt Enterprises, not for Oak Hills. And now? Are you still doing all of this for me?"

"In a way, everything is for you, but to answer your question, no. I like toiling with your dad in the vineyards, working with your mom on the harvest dinner, putting together the contest. But I still want you. I've never met such a beautiful, clever, capable control freak I like more than you." He covered her hand with his on the table.

She snorted, studying him with rapt attention.

He would have given all he owned to hear the thoughts going through her head.

She weaved her fingers through his, giving them a tender squeeze. "I want you, too."

He whistled. "That is a great answer."

"But I don't know anything about you. Not really." She drew back.

"What are you talking about? You know more about me than almost any other person."

She slumped in her chair. "Your relationships are really that shallow?"

Hurt, heavy and hard, bore down on him. He couldn't deny her words no matter how much he wanted to.

"I'm sorry, I didn't mean that as a nasty comment. The concept of not knowing someone well is outside of my world. Serenity Creek is such a small town. You're acquainted with everyone and their history pretty much back to when they were born. Maybe that's why dating has been so difficult. I've grown up with all the men in town. I'm way more informed than I want to be about them."

He should tell her the reason had more to do with her priorities, but pushing that subject would get him nowhere.

"I've told you about me. What else is there to tell you?"

"You never talk about your mom."

Instant pain ripped through him. No, anything but that.

He looked at her, slits of shadows and candlelight skipping across her face, entreating him.

He put his utensils aside, grabbed his glass and took a long sip before telling the story that had never crossed his lips.

"My mom died when I was ten."

She gasped. "I'm sorry. I had no idea. No wonder you don't like talking about it."

He had to say it at some point and perhaps telling her out loud would relieve the constant ache in him.

"She was amazing. Your mom reminds me a lot of her. Supportive to a fault, loving, a great cook."

"You got your love of food from her, then?"

He nodded, still smelling the rich chocolate of the first batch of brownies they had made together. "My mom and I cooked together constantly. In reality, she was a single parent even though she was married to Clayton, but she cared enough about me for both of them. Then, she got sick. Clayton hired a private nurse and a nanny, paid for all of her treatments, and kept right on working from the office. He stopped by only a handful of times to see me or check in on her. When she died from complications, my father brought me to his New York penthouse with the nanny. It wasn't long before he shipped me off to boarding school, which may have been better for both of us since I couldn't stand the sight of him by then."

"It must have been awful for you."

"Being in small towns reminds me of her and the one we lived in."

He caught an almost imperceptible wince from her.

"So that's why you're not a fan of small towns."

If only it were that simple. He'd launched into his story, might as well tell her all of it.

"Yes and no. Small towns remind me of my mom, but also of the people who lived in that place with us."

"What are you talking about?"

"When my mom died, when I could have used a little support, a kind word, all I got from our neighbors and everyone else in that spit of land were questions about how I was feeling, what was going to happen to me now, if I wanted to come live with them."

She wrinkled her eyebrows. "Wait, I'm confused, those sound like good things."

"And they would have been if they meant them to help me. Any answer I gave ended up on the front page of some tabloid and I overheard a few of them talking to Clayton about taking me in for a substantial amount of money on a yearly basis."

"I can't believe they would do such a thing. That's terrible."

"Bet you're glad you asked about the real me." He twirled his wine glass, images of his mother, those ridiculous residents, and his father all swirling around together. "

"I am. I like you, all of you, a lot. Is that why … " she paused. "Is that why you've never stayed put? You never grew up with a home life so you have no idea what having one would be like?"

He rubbed his jaw. "I've never thought about it, Freud. It's possible."

"It's not so bad once you get used to it."

"Are you offering?"

She stared at him, her eyes wide. "We should clean up. It's getting late."

She rose, stacking up plates and silverware.

Not the words he had hoped she would say.

"Why is it you never ask me about myself?" she asked as they carried everything over to the sink.

He had read all about her online, but his real source had much more information on her than the Internet. "Your mom. She filled me in on your life story over home-baked strudel and coffee."

"Of course. Well, I still have secrets."

"Prove it."

"Uh-uh. I'm not giving them up that easily."

"I think it's only fair after I shared mine."

She sighed. "What hasn't my mom told you?"

"She said you were almost engaged once, but she wouldn't say anything more."

The mystery had triggered all sorts of possible scenarios in his mind until he had almost made some calls to find out on his own. But sneaking around behind her back for news, besides asking her mother, wouldn't have earned him any points with her.

"I'm glad she still has some loyalty to me."

"Plenty." He waited silently for her to continue and when she didn't offer up anything else prompted, "So?"

"So what? Yes, I came close to getting engaged. To a city dweller like you. No, I'm not going to tell you about it. Not tonight."

"That's something, at least. I guess. Not tonight would infer that you'll tell me some time in the future. Preferably the near future?"

One corner of her lip curved up. "Maybe, Colt, maybe."

He knew better than to push her. She'd tell him when she was ready. He'd make sure of it.

They made quick work of loading up the dishwasher, and far too soon Madison escorted him to the door. He didn't want the night to end, not yet.

He turned to face her. "I'm sorry I forced you to go kayaking."

She shrugged. "Don't be. I'm not. I liked it."

"Even though you almost drowned?"

He didn't want to think about what could have happened, refused to even fathom it.

"Stop being melodramatic. I hardly came close to drowning."

"Too close for my comfort." He snatched her wrist, tugging her against him. "There's something I've been wanting to do all day."

Tipping her chin up, he kissed her, weaving his other hand through her hair as she slid her fingers down his back in slow motion, creating a trail of fire wherever she touched. It burned straight through his heart. He had to put himself on the line, see if she would go out with him for him, not a job.

He pulled away, hovering over her.

"Have dinner with me. A real date. Nothing to do with business, only us," he said, his voice rough and hoarse.

She dragged in a breath. "On one condition."

"Name it."

"I get to pick where we go and it's going to be a surprise. It's my turn after all of your secret excursions. And don't expect anything extravagant."

"Never. Perfect plan." He touched his forehead to hers.

Funny how a low key date with her sounded like just that. Perfect—even with the barbed wire fences she put up around herself when it came to him and their different backgrounds. He hoped to break those down piece by piece. Next to that, dealing with her overprotective, annoying brother would be easy. The hurdle that most troubled him, though, would be anything but simple, and it had nothing to do with Madison and everything to do with his own battles.

# CHAPTER ELEVEN

Madison dug in her closet, throwing shirt after shirt over her shoulder.

"I'm getting bombarded over here. Can you ease up a little?" Tessa asked.

"Sorry. I've been having trouble making clothing decisions as of late."

Madison sat on the floor, taking in the sight of her friend encircled with clothes and flinging shirts off her head.

"I still think the blue sundress with the denim jacket is the way to go."

Madison scrunched up her nose. "You don't think it will be too fancy? Tonight is about being casual. Or should I go for extravagant? Would he like that better?"

"Either one. Because it's become more about being with him than where you are, right?"

Madison blinked in silence. This pinpointed the exact reason she had called Tessa over today. No one else could calm her down, refocus her mind, and help her pick out the perfect outfit at the same time.

"Yes," Madison answered.

"It's the same thing with your outfit. It doesn't matter what you wear; what matters is spending time with Jake."

Madison hopped up and jumped onto the bed, clothes flying everywhere, to hug Tessa.

"I'm so glad you came over."

Tessa laughed. "Of course. I haven't seen you call in for back up to get ready to go out with a guy since high school. No way was I going to miss this."

In truth, Madison hadn't experienced this level of excitement flowing through her veins since her first date.

"Where did the blue sundress go?" Madison picked apart the pile of garments around her, scanning the floor as well.

Tessa also started in on the search. "So what did Adam say when you told him that Jake almost drowned you yesterday and now you're going out with him?"

"Jake didn't drown me, he saved me. And Adam said he had something to take care of before hanging up on me."

Tessa sucked in a breath. "Are you sure Jake's still going to be alive for your date?"

"He can handle Adam. Better than any of my other dates from what I've seen."

Tessa snorted. "That's for sure. Tucker's lucky to still be breathing. But how are you holding up? Are you and Adam still at odds?"

"He's my brother; we're always at odds when it comes to my dating life, always have been since he figures no one's ever good enough for me. We still love each other, though. I think we're both aware of how a man in my life could change our relationship and vice versa with a woman in his. He has my best interests at heart. He'll come around."

"I found it," Tessa announced, presenting Madison with the sapphire-blue sleeveless dress.

Madison grabbed it. "Perfect. Thank you."

"No problem."

Madison pulled off her top and unzipped her jeans, tossing both aside.

Tessa folded a shirt. "Be honest, how do you feel about Jake? Is it still awkward that he bought the family business? Doesn't it bother you, all those women he's gone out with?"

"I'm not sure if I'll ever be comfortable with him owning Oak Hills, but he's been doing great things for the winery. Dad told me he's been learning a ton and asking lots of questions. He's even had some ideas to improve the wines themselves that Dad thinks have real merit to them, which is saying something. He might not be as irresponsible as I originally thought." Madison shrugged. "And who can really trust the media when it comes to gossip, especially about a person's love life?"

Tessa nodded her head once in a conceding manner. "True enough. I only hope he's worthy of you, which I assume he is or you wouldn't have agreed to an actual date."

"Thank you for trusting my judgment. Adam should take a lesson from you."

"It's different when you're in the brother role. His head's too clouded with date defense strategies to think clearly."

Madison giggled, adjusting the tiny blue belt that cinched the dress's fabric around her waist. She turned in a circle. "What do you think?"

"You look amazing. Do you want me to put your hair up?"

"No, I'm going to leave it down. I could use some assistance with makeup, though."

"Sure. But what do you think about a pre-dinner drink? I brought a bottle of Gianini chardonnay. I thought it might settle your nerves."

"I'll never turn down some of your wine."

Tessa left the room, heading to the kitchen.

Madison put her hand on her tummy. Butterflies. But not like she'd had on their other excursions. Those had been from worry about what awaited her. Doubt fluttered these butterflies. Was she repeating past mistakes? Only one way to find out, and she wouldn't miss her chance.

She turned on her curling iron, checking her watch. He should be here in less than a half hour. Barring any altercations with Adam, of course, and assuming he survived.

• • •

Jake splashed water on his face, washing away the remnants of his shaving cream, and toweled off when a series of loud thuds pounded on the door to his room.

"Just a minute," he called out.

He strode across the floor, barefooted and in his jeans. He didn't bother putting on a shirt as the incessant knocking continued.

Who could be making such a ruckus and why?

He threw open the door and saw Adam standing there aiming a fierce glare straight at him.

Great. He knew what that look meant.

Jake leaned against the frame. "Do you want to do this outside or in the bar?"

Outside would mean using fists, inside would be with words. Either way, things were bound to get brutal.

"Let's start in the bar. We can move things outside if necessary," Adam growled.

"Fine. I'll meet you downstairs in five minutes."

Adam turned and marched down the hallway without a single word or move to acknowledge him.

Jake shut the door, smothering the anger mounting in him. Getting into it with Madison's brother wouldn't endear him to her.

He pulled on a white polo shirt and snatched up his jacket, swinging it over his shoulder. He tucked his cell phone, wallet, and keys into his pockets, combed his fingers through his hair, and headed out to meet with Madison's gatekeeper.

As soon as he entered the dimly lit bar in the inn, he spotted Adam on a barstool, talking it up with the bartender as if he had known the guy since childhood, which considering the size of the town, he probably did. A similar story applied to half the residents around here, so if things went south between him and Madison, they would all close ranks against him, and he had a feeling his wealth and stature wouldn't mean a thing to them then.

He made his way past the tables just beginning to fill with customers and sat next to Adam as the bartender excused himself. Two whiskies already sat on the bar for them.

"I thought this talk required something more manly than wine."

"I agree," Jake said, trying to gauge Adam's manner and getting a sense of where things stood.

Neither of them touched the shots.

"First off, I want to thank you for saving Madison yesterday."

Jake bowed his head, surprise fusing with caution.

"Secondly," Adam put up two fingers, his face contorting in fury, "what were you thinking taking her kayaking on the open ocean? Are you nuts? I'm sure she told you she's not a great swimmer."

"You're right. I made a bad decision." He couldn't deny what he'd been beating himself up about since it happened. "I wanted her to get out from behind her camera to experience what she photographs so beautifully. I didn't expect the dolphins to come that close. I'm not saying this as an excuse. I take full responsibility for what occurred. Believe me, I would never let anything happen to her."

His intense need to protect her rivaled Adam's countenance.

Adam stared at him. "I had planned a long, angry lecture, but I can't after what you said. I was really looking forward to it, too."

"I'm sorry to disappoint."

"I've heard from my dad that you've come up with a few good ideas for the wines and have been implementing much needed updates to the winery."

The rapid change in subject was definitely confusing. "I've managed some improvements here and there."

"And I appreciate you letting my sister plan where you guys go tonight. It won't be anything extravagant. She's not into the ritzy scene."

Jake grunted. "So she told me. She's very good at making her opinion known."

Adam smiled, pride shining in his eyes. "That's my Maddy."

That was Jake's spitfire.

Adam folded his hands on the bar. "This is the deal. I back up my sister no matter what. If she decides to continue dating you, I'll support her—not necessarily you, but hers and your relationship. You might get an equal benefit if you stick around long enough to earn it. But if you hurt Maddy in any way, I'll make certain you wish you'd never landed one wheel in this town. Agreed?" Adam offered him his hand.

Jake studied his determined expression and capable build. Adam wasn't one to be crossed, but then neither was he. From what he could tell if things went wrong with Madison—which he hoped they wouldn't but both of them had enough baggage to rival the cargo load of a commercial airplane—a fistfight with Adam would ensue and get him more bruises than his first skiing accident. Not that Adam would fare much better.

But it was a ceasefire all the same.

He shook Adam's hand. "Agreed. I don't want to offend Madison any more than you want to see her offended."

"Should we drink to it?" Adam asked, grabbing his whiskey.

"Of course."

Adam raised his glass. "To Maddy."

"To Madison." Jake clinked his glass with Adam's before they both threw back the shots in one swallow.

• • •

Jake bounded up the stairs to Madison's apartment, taking them two at a time. He reached his arm to knock on the door when it opened, revealing Madison and another woman with brown hair he didn't recognize.

"Jake, you made it," Madison said, relief washing over her face.

"You had a doubt?" he asked.

"No." Madison shook her head. "This is my best friend, Tessa Gianini. Tessa, this is Jake Colt."

"It's nice to finally meet you," Tessa said.

"The pleasure is mine. I've had the privilege of meeting your mother."

"So I heard. I'm sorry."

"Don't be. She has a good heart."

Tessa's eyebrows shot up and she leaned closer to Madison, whispering, "Are you sure he's real?"

Jake chuckled. "I've read a lot about the Gianini winery and heard all the rave reviews about the father-daughter winemaking duo there. From what I hear, you have a pretty large operation going, including a café and everything."

"Thank you. It's not big enough that it can't be family run." Tessa shrugged. "My older sister runs the café, my younger one handles the tasting room with my mom, and my dad and I take care of the wines. You'll have to come over and see our property sometime."

"Isn't that like scoping out the competition?"

She laughed. "Not around here. We're all in this together." She hugged Madison from the side. "Call me later." Tessa waved as she squeezed past him and down the stairs.

"Are you ready?" he asked, taking great appreciation in the snug blue dress skimming over Madison's body.

"Yes."

He slipped his fingers through hers as they made their way to the car. "Where are we going?"

"To a little pizza place called Pomadora's. There's a fantastic ice cream shop around the corner from it so I figured we could grab dessert there."

"Pizza and ice cream. Sounds great."

The drive to Pomadora's Pizza Parlor took less then ten minutes. He parked on the street in front of the restaurant and opened the door for her.

As soon as they walked in, an elderly couple rushed up to them, all warmth and smiles.

"*Tesoro*, it's good to see you and you brought a handsome man this time. You'll eat here tonight, yes?" the woman asked, embracing Madison in a crushing hug.

"Yes, Mama Pomadora," Madison answered and then motioned to him. "This is Jake Colt. Jake, this is Mama Pomadora and her husband, Albirto."

He shook hands with the couple. "It's a pleasure to meet you both."

Albirto led them through the small restaurant jam packed with patrons who were busy chatting and devouring the hot pizza before them. A few curious stares came their way, but Jake had become so accustomed to them, he hardly noticed anymore.

"Some wine, perhaps?" Albirto asked, seating them a table for two at the back of the room under a black-and-white photograph of Mama Pomadora in the kitchen, flour on her apron as she tossed a disc of dough in the air.

Madison gave Jake an expectant expression.

He gestured to her. "This is your night. You decide."

She grinned. "Thank you. We'll have a bottle of the Oak Hills syrah."

"Of course. I'll have your waiter bring it to you." Albirto left them alone.

Jake set his menu aside. "So what's Mama Pomadora's real name? It can't be Mama Pomadora."

She rested her chin on her palm. "I have no idea."

"How long has this place been here?"

"Since I can remember. We used to come here at least once a week when Adam and I were in elementary school. We loved pizza nights."

"Looks like you still do." He hitched his thumb at the picture on the wall. "Did you take that?"

"No, but I wish I did. It's an older photograph. The angle is perfect and it captures the moment so well." She pointed at the menu he had set next to his plate. "You're not hungry?"

"I'm a guy. I'm starving. And who wouldn't be with the smells coming out of that kitchen?"

Garlic, basil, and fresh baked dough tormented him.

"Then, why aren't you perusing the menu?"

"I already told you. This is your night. You're making all the decisions. Complete control."

A month ago he would have found the idea of giving anyone power over himself impossible, but not in this situation, not with her. He trusted her enough to follow her decisions, her guidance. Not that he couldn't or wouldn't make calls on his own, only that he liked sharing them with her.

"I don't want complete control."

"You? Are you kidding?"

"I'm serious. I admit I did, and I still think you've been managing every minute we've been together. But things are a little different now. I'm getting used to your choices. You're the chef, what do you like on your pizza?"

"Everything."

"Good. Me, too. We'll get the works."

Their waiter came with the bottle of syrah and took their order.

She picked up her glass, sipping the cherry red wine. "What's the next big escapade we're undertaking to photograph?"

"Nothing. No more adventures to market." He took a large gulp of the smooth wine to settle the apprehension crawling around his gut.

He hoped she would understand.

Her shoulders sank, her cheeks paled, and she stared at him with unblinking eyes. "What do you mean? That's it? That's all? Does your decision have anything to do with yesterday in the water?"

"Partly."

"I'm up for more."

He snorted. "You may be, but I'm not. I can't risk something more serious happening to you."

She leaned forward, a sly smile curving her lips. "The city dweller can't handle our rough outdoors?"

"This city dweller is no match for you."

She had won, had infiltrated all his thoughts and emotions, and he loved every bit of it even if he hadn't a clue where things could possibly go between them.

She circled the rim of her glass with her finger. "Nothing could be farther from the truth and we both know it. I wouldn't have made it through anything without you. You can't really mean we won't have more photo sessions."

The waiter returned with a steaming pizza buried under a mountain of meats and vegetables. He set it between them and shaved some fresh Parmesan cheese over the top before excusing himself.

Jake tore off two slices for each of them and made sure to leave his fork and knife where they sat, digging in with his hands as she did. "Very good. You'll have to try the pizza in New York sometime."

"Fat chance."

"Worth a shot." He took another bite. "It's not just about keeping you safe. I still think it's important for you to experience all life has to offer. The harvest festival is starting next week, though, and that will keep us both busy. Not to mention that, thanks to you, we have a wide array of photos to choose from already, and I need to get the brochures, website, and other marketing material updated and put out there. I'll need your help setting all that up so no, we're not done working together, not in the least. I want to see you for personal reasons, though, not just for business."

She smiled. "I'd like that, too."

"I knew we could agree on something."

"You've really been getting into the whole harvest thing. Dad said the wine tasting tables you ordered are going to be a big hit, and you've been a tremendous help in getting everything ready for the tourists. Mom can't stop talking about you, period."

Something he hadn't experienced since college coiled through him. Pride in his own work.

"I love dealing with your parents."

She sipped her wine. "And the winery?"

"The winery, too."

"And me?"

"Especially you."

"Good answer."

He poured more wine into their glasses. "It's the only one I could give without lying."

She giggled. "I take it back."

"Take what back?"

"You are charming."

"Was there ever any reservation?" He helped himself to more pizza, setting another slice on her plate. "I'm glad you've changed your mind." Very glad.

"Me, too."

He relaxed into the restaurant's ambiance and the easy conversation with her. The meal passed faster than he wished and before he knew it, their waiter came back with mints. But no check.

"Pardon me, where's the bill?" he asked as politely as he could in such a situation.

"It's been taken care of already, sir," their waiter answered, pivoting to walk to the kitchen.

Madison sent him a mischievous smile. "I paid for everything ahead of time with Mama Pomadora's approval."

He knew beyond a doubt that his jaw had just hit the floor. "What? Why would you do that?"

"It's my turn to treat you."

No woman had ever purchased anything for him. The action unsettled him. He understood what it meant to her, though, especially considering her budget constraints and desperate need to stand on her own two feet.

"You didn't have to, but thank you. I appreciate it." He stood up and held her jacket for her as she slid her arms in. "I think you promised me ice cream and that's on me. No complaints."

She giggled. "Deal. And it's not just ice cream, it's wonderful, knock-your-socks-off ice cream."

He followed her out the door.

A brisk breeze hit them as they stepped into the cool fall evening. A full moon lit their path.

They strode down the street and she snuggled up against him.

She belonged here in his arms. He couldn't deny the certainty of it or how much he relished having her next to him.

By far she had been the least expensive date he had ever had and the best. He would rather sit with her for hours on end in a hole-in-the-wall pizza joint than eat with anyone else in the most fashionable restaurant in New York.

At the end of the day, though, where did that leave a city dweller and a country girl?

• • •

Madison accepted the strawberry ice cream cone the young girl behind the counter presented her and took a delectable bite while she waited for Jake to get his chocolate ice cream.

"Should we eat in here or do you want to keep walking?" he asked, sampling the tower of chocolate in his hand.

She scanned the bright room scattered with empty bistro tables. "Let's keep strolling along. The night's too beautiful to stay inside."

"All right." Jake offered her his arm. "This is great ice cream, by the way."

"I told you." She linked her arm through his, licking a melting dribble of pink cream from her cone. "You'll have to keep me warm, though."

He chuckled, lowering his head to whisper in her ear. "Not a problem."

His heat traveled from her head to her toes as she nestled closer to him.

Lampposts lit the sidewalk along with the moonlight cascading down upon the town. A few other couples milled about around them.

She couldn't believe how much she'd enjoyed this night, the time with him. He didn't seem as different in her world anymore.

"What made you get into flying?" she asked.

It was still the one thing she could never contemplate embracing.

"I fly all over the place. Sometimes on commercial airlines … "

"You fly commercial? No way."

He cocked his head. "Sometimes, yes."

"First class?"

"Does it matter?"

"First class. Keep going."

So what if he spent more on a plane ticket than she spent in rent for one month. He wasn't showing off or waving it in her face. He never had, and he deserved a lot more credit for that than she had given him.

"Other times I fly on one of Colt Enterprises's jets. I thought it might be fun to give it a try myself so I took some classes and found I'd rather be in the cockpit than the passenger seat any day. There's nothing to do in the backseat but sit there and go wherever the pilot takes you. Not like when I'm flying my MD 600N and the sky is literally the limit."

He didn't want to be told what do to, not even in transportation. He'd had enough of that from his father, no doubt. So as much as she wanted to tell him to stay, to keep working with her parents at Oak Hills she couldn't, even if she thought a remote chance existed that he would listen to her. He had to make the decision on his own, just as she had changed her mind, her unrelenting belief that her mission was to force him to leave town.

Her life had turned upside down all over again. But would it be for the better?

"Where have you flown exactly?"

"Too many countries to count. Clayton loves buying up properties all over the world, tearing them down, and putting up something grander and more profitable in their place."

"The world? I can't imagine … " She stopped short as his words sank in. "Wait, what do you mean he tears them down? Is that what he wants to do with Oak Hills?"

Fear wrung her gut.

He lowered his head. "Madison … "

"It is, isn't it? He can't. He can't do it." Her heart leapt into her throat, thickening her speech.

"No, he can't, and I won't let him. He's agreed to try something different. I told him he had to if he wanted me to handle the project. We're going to turn things around. Together." He pulled her in closer.

She sank into him and the same trust she felt when he dragged her out of the water wrapped itself around her like a cocoon. "Thank you," she whispered.

The realization that he, and he alone, stood between his father and the total annihilation of Oak Hills hit her like a sucker punch.

He had fought for them. The last remnants of her restraint, of her carefully composed logic for denying her feelings for him and not repeating the mistakes of her past slipped through her grasp.

All the effort he was putting into the winery was his own decision, no one else's. Maybe he had found his passion after all. But did he realize it?

"Anytime." He nuzzled her hair. "Maybe in return you can tell me about your almost engagement. What happened?"

She sighed, accepting the inevitability of sharing the tale with him. "Same old story. Boy meets girl, boy makes promises he can't keep then leaves girl when his career shoots forward."

"I don't think that's how it usually goes."

"Well, that's how this one went. Tucker White, said boy, came into Serenity Creek as a reformed—supposedly—city dweller. He'd just lost his job at a law firm that was downsizing and came here for a vacation. We ran into each other at The Wine Cork, literally, and were inseparable ever since."

"I don't like the guy already. Of course, I haven't liked the guy since I heard you were almost engaged to him."

She laughed, the pressure on her chest easing. "I don't like him very much anymore, either. We dated for about a year while he took odd jobs here in town and talked about opening up a law firm, getting married, buying a house, kids. All the things he knew I wanted to hear. By the time we started looking at rings, I was convinced he was perfect and that city people actually could live in small towns and become one of us."

His hand tensed around her. The gesture was slight yet unmistakable.

"He arranged a romantic dinner for us at his place, but instead of popping the question, he told me he'd been offered a new job at a swanky law firm in L.A., complete with an extravagant salary. He was leaving in a few days and asked me to go with him. Just like that, up and leave my whole family, everything I've worked for, in a matter of days. I knew in my heart I didn't want to go, but we had invested in a relationship and I wanted to be fair to him, so I asked him to give me some time to think about. I helped him pack up and promised to visit him so we could discuss our plans. I thought we could make it work somehow."

"But you never visited him?"

She hated retelling this movie, a dark, twisted film with a bad ending that she had seen in her head too many times. The hurt had dulled with time, but the truths she had learned remained strong. "Oh, I did. It took a little while because every time I mentioned it, he was too busy with work to see me. Even on the weekends. Finally, I just decided to surprise him."

"I'm assuming it didn't go well?" The gentleness of his voice mingled with his teasing in a priceless combination of support.

"That's an understatement. I finally found his apartment after getting lost for an hour on the maze of freeways down there. I was still in time, though, to see him with his new, rich model girlfriend. It wasn't a long conversation because as I stood there speechless while he explained that he needed someone with the right background and connections to share his ride to the top, not some backward country bumpkin."

Of all the things Tucker had done, his words that day had stung the most, and she still carried them around within her like shrapnel from an explosion.

"What an idiot. He didn't deserve you. Not a minute of your time. You know that, right?" He kissed the top of her head.

"Now. What he got and he deserved, though, were very different. I spent the next couple of hours after that argument wondering the streets of L.A. with no idea where I was going and feeling completely lost, both literally and figuratively, in a jumble of car horns and people rushing everywhere. I hit a bad part of town and got mugged."

"What?" He held her closer as if protecting her from the attack that had occurred so long ago.

"Yup. They stole my purse, shoved me aside, and took off. Never got caught. Good thing I had kept my keys in my pocket or I wouldn't have had a way out of that nightmarish place. Of course, when I finally found my car, I had a parking ticket."

Whistling, he said, "I see where your dislike of cities comes from."

"And men from those cities." She looked up and met his eyes. "I'm making an exception for you."

She hoped he understood how big of an exception it was, how much it meant to her.

He stopped, turning her toward him. "You have a little ice cream on your face."

"I do?" She raised her fingers to her face, but he caught them in his grasp before they could reach it.

"I'll get it."

He brushed away the cool stickiness on her cheek, leaning in to kiss her lips. He tugged her in close and she molded her body to his.

All her thoughts faded, all her concerns. Their differences and the slew of pictures she had seen of him with other women didn't matter because right then, right there she was the only woman with him under the moonlight in Serenity Creek. She'd deal with whatever the consequences tomorrow.

# CHAPTER TWELVE

Madison stretched like a contented cat under her grandmother's quilt as the morning sun broke into her room with a golden sheen. She couldn't wait to see Jake again.

Her phone buzzed and she noted Tessa's name on the caller ID.

"Hey, how did last night go?" Tessa asked, her voice low and not as enthusiastic as she had expected.

"It was beyond wonderful. I had such a great time with him, Tess. It was so romantic even with the casual dinner. I'm seriously walking on air right now."

"Then you haven't seen the paper this morning. Or you're taking this whole thing really well."

Madison shot up in bed. "What are you talking about?"

"Listen, don't look at any papers until you get coffee. Meet me at Lily's. It's definitely on me."

Dread drenched her like a cold shower. "I'm on my way."

"See you soon."

Madison hung up, throwing aside her covers and launching herself from the bed. She rushed around the room, throwing on a pair of jeans and a light sweater and shoving her hair into a ponytail. Not bothering with makeup, she rinsed her face, brushed her teeth, and grabbed her purse to leave.

She drove to Lily's, a sickening sensation churning in her belly. Arriving early, she parked her beat-up car on the street. No sign of Tessa yet.

The moment she entered the coffeehouse, the bustle slowed to murmurs and curious glances came her way. She ducked her head and went straight for the newspaper twand. Forget the coffee.

She snatched a copy of the regional newspaper, feeling dizzy as she read the headline. A picture of her and Jake kissing on the sidewalk sprang out at her under the title "Playboy Jake Colt's Newest Flavor of the Month, Madison Carmichael."

"I tried to warn you to get coffee first," Tessa said, coming up behind her. She scrutinized the curious onlookers around them. "Maybe meeting in public wasn't the best idea. Why don't you go to your car, and I'll join you there with liquid reinforcements."

Lily came up next to them on the other side of the counter. "I'll get your usual order ready to go. If there's anything I can do to help, just ask."

The sympathy in Lily's eyes undid her.

Madison nodded, mumbling a thank you and marched out the door to the safety of her car.

She hunkered in the driver's seat, hiding her face behind the paper and forcing herself to read each word of the scathing article. It talked about Jake's notoriety with women and the short lifespan of his relationships, how she was the latest in a long line of females he had enjoyed himself with and she would not be the last.

She read the final sentence, the one describing Jake's role as the new owner of fledging local winery, Oak Hills, and how short his visit here would be. It didn't take long for it to sink in.

She stared ahead, blind to everything on the street and numb to her bones.

Against her better judgment, she snuck a peek back at the large picture of her and Jake. Being on the receiving end of a camera was bad enough—having the photo scattered across the front page for all to see was like standing in the middle of town naked with a blinking, neon sign pointing at her.

Tessa opened the passenger side door, sliding into the seat next to her. "Okay, extra large coffees. Lily threw in some chocolate croissants on the house. She said you looked like you could use some chocolate in addition to caffeine."

Tessa passed her a warm to-go cup and a small, white bag holding the promised croissant.

Madison swallowed a fortifying gulp of coffee. Its heat seared a path down her throat.

So these were the costs she had to confront for her date with Jake. She couldn't run from them. She had to tackle them. With chocolate and loads of caffeine. She clutched her cup in a death grip and bit into the flaky pastry. "Say something," Tessa urged.

What could she say? The article threw Jake's cavalier attitude toward dating in her face, and put her on the same level as all the other women he had been with, the exact place she had determined never to be. Not to mention the reporter referenced Jake leaving soon, an even scarier notion than his string of past girlfriends.

But she knew him better now than the press. Didn't she? Maybe something more existed between her and Jake than a nonpermanent relationship. She couldn't deny that's what she wanted. And yet, she'd had the same thoughts about Tucker, and look where that false hope had gotten her. Tucker had told her she didn't belong to the same social strata as him, and Jake hailed from an even higher echelon than Tucker. All of Jake's previous girlfriends came from his world, so what did that mean for her?

She took a deep breath. "It's just the local newspaper. It doesn't cover that much territory. I'm sure we're both overreacting."

Tessa bit her lip. Her eyes darted down to the pile of papers on her lap.

"What?" Madison asked, recoiling against the seat.

"Well … " Tessa started, casting another glance at the stack resting on her legs.

Madison looked hard at the newspapers. "Oh, no. Don't tell me."

"I'm afraid so. I had a bad feeling after seeing the front page of the paper, so I stopped by the market on the way over here. A similar story with the same photograph is in all the major tabloids."

Madison groaned.

Tessa sipped her latte. "It gets worse."

"How could it possibly get worse?"

"They mention your photography business in most articles."

"Excuse me?" Madison barely breathed the words.

Tessa rushed on. "It could be a good thing. They don't say anything bad about your pictures, just that you're trying to get your business going. These are national publications. Think of the exposure."

"I don't need everyone in the country to know I'm struggling to get things going, and I want my business to be recognized for my talents, not for dating Jake."

She should hightail it out of whatever she had started with Jake, retreat into the safety of her contained, structured life, and refocus on building her dream, on her own. But was that what she really wanted?

Her cell phone blared, startling her out of her reverie. She hazarded a hesitant glance at the caller ID, uncertain what she would do if she saw Jake's name.

"Hey, Mom," she answered, signaling to Tessa to wait a moment.

"Hey, sweetie. We need your help. Can you please come over this afternoon to assist with tastings? We had a lot of extra traffic yesterday, thanks to all of the publicity work Jake has done, and today should be even busier. Adam will be here and Jake said he'd make it as well."

Her heart skipped a beat at the thought of seeing Jake again. Between their date and the media, everything had changed between them now.

"Of course, I'll be there."

Madison hung up and broke off another large bite of croissant. Obviously her mother hadn't seen the articles, or she had chosen to ignore them.

She swallowed hard. "I have to go. I have some pictures for the winery I need to edit before I head on over to Oak Hills."

"Sure. I should get back myself. I have loads to get done before we open. This harvest festival has had a much stronger showing than years past."

"Yup."

"And that would be because of Jake, wouldn't it?"

No denying it.

"Yup."

Tessa sighed. She stretched across the center console to hug Madison. "Call me later and remember, I'm always here for you."

"Thanks."

Madison set her cup down as Tessa left the car to walk to her own.

She let her head fall against the steering wheel for a second, sinking into the tight tangle of frustration, embarrassment, and fear threatening her. But only for an instant. Then she shoved it all away, started the car after a couple of tries, and drove to her apartment. She'd have to deal with Jake and the articles later; right now she had work to do and she hoped with utter desperation that she could bury herself in it to avoid the main worry nagging her. What would the press coverage and this thing with Jake mean for Oak Hills and her family?

•••

Jake stormed through the hotel lobby, the local paper rolled up in his fist. The morning had started off so well and then it had plunged straight down after he saw the front page of the paper over breakfast in the hotel restaurant.

He could hear the same whispers and see the sidelong looks he always received when a story about his love life got splashed across the media. This time, though, an undercurrent of protectiveness passed through the air around him. Not for him—that much was obvious from the tsking he had received from an older woman. They guarded Madison.

He barely broke his stride long enough for the doorman to open the door for him.

"Good morning, Mr. Colt."

"Good morning, Henry," he grumbled.

"Nice girl, that Madison Carmichael. We all love her, want the best for her, you know?"

Yeah, he knew all right. He knew that Henry and half the town would join forces with Adam in a flash to knock his lights out if he put so much as one toe over the line they had drawn. He'd heard similar comments earlier this morning.

He restrained the rage boiling inside him.

"So do I, Henry, so do I."

He couldn't imagine his hometown defending him with such fierce devotion. They'd been quick to throw him to the wolves. But when push came to shove, was one small town really so different than another?

If the article had been published at any other time, he'd have figured someone in Serenity Creek had sold him out. Not everyone could be an angel around here.

He marched up to the Range Rover, threw open the door and climbed inside, slamming the door with so much force it rocked the car.

He had always hated the press and their constant coverage of the women he dated, but this article took his fury to another level. No doubt the tabloids had picked up the same story.

The thought of Madison being turned into a trophy, just one among the many others, punched him in the gut, sucking all the air from his lungs. She meant more to him than a mere fling and he never wanted anyone to think less of her.

His phone buzzed with Clayton's name appearing on the screen. He hit the ignore button and stashed his phone in the cup holder, before turning to start the engine.

He checked the time on the dashboard. He was supposed to be at Oak Hills helping with the crowds, but he needed to set the record straight first. He'd have to be late.

•••

Madison ran up the dirt road to the winery. She had parked far away to leave room for the tourists' cars and then discovered she wouldn't have been able to find a parking spot close by even if she had tried. The lot was full and cars lined the street. The whole place bustled with people.

She didn't slow down until she almost collided with Adam outside the back entrance to the winery.

"Whoops," she said, catching her breath.

He hoisted up a case of pinot noir. "You're late."

"Car trouble."

"You really need a new car."

"What is it with everyone saying I need a new car?" She pointed at the crate he carried. "Did a customer buy that?"

"Well they aren't stealing it."

"That's great." She held up her hand for a high five. Jake's marketing and connections had paid off.

"So you may be famous now and all, but are you ready to help?" Adam teased.

She cringed. "You saw the paper?"

"Everyone saw it, Maddy. Don't worry, you looked beautiful."

She rolled her eyes. "That's the least of my concerns. I'm not sure what to make of the article."

He shrugged. "You'll figure it out. Whatever you decide, I'm behind you a hundred percent. I had a man-to-man talk with Jake yesterday, so he knows where things stand. If you don't like the article, I can beat him up for you. I can even whack him upside the head with the paper in question."

She laughed, the action relieving the pressure on her chest.

Adam had always been her rock, his support unwavering and unending. "I'm sure you would and I'm thankful for it, but, no, I don't want you to fight Jake."

"That's convenient, because I'm kind of starting to respect the guy."

"Really? I'm glad to hear that."

"But, Maddy, in all seriousness, you are too special to be considered just another good time."

She rose up on her toes to kiss his cheek. "Thank you." She cleared her throat. "Speaking of Jake, is he here?"

He shook his head. "No."

Disappointment clung to her. "But I heard he was working today."

"He's not here. Maybe he's coming later."

"Sure. I should find Mom and see where she needs me."

Why hadn't Jake shown up yet? Would he bail on them in favor of something more exciting? Was there any truth to what the article had said about him leaving soon?

The notion that he could be every bit as irresponsible as she had considered him at the start of this mess wound itself through her like poison, and she clung to the antidote of trust with as firm a grip as she could muster.

She found her mother in the cellar, counting bottles of chardonnay.

"Sweetie, thank goodness you're here." Rose pulled her in for a hurried embrace.

"Sorry for being late."

"No problem. We're happy you could even come. Your dad and I are busy getting things organized for the harvest dinner, so do you mind supervising the tasting room and manning the counter? Adam's already up there."

"Of course. Mom, about the paper this morning."

"Don't believe everything you read."

"What about the winery?"

Her mother pointed at the door leading to the front. "Did you see all the cars and people? We're not hurting, sweetie. I have to go. Don't worry about it."

Rose left the room, leaving her alone in the cellar.

She shrugged, stashing her purse next to a wine rack and heading to the tasting room.

A cacophony of chatter and clinking glasses assailed her as soon as she stepped into the crowded space. People milled about the room, exploring the wines and snacks available for purchase while a pack of customers swarmed the bar area for tastings.

She spotted Adam helping some customers decide on the right cheese to go with the chardonnay they had purchased while a couple of temp workers they had used in the past were already serving at the bar.

With resignation, she rolled up her sleeves and slid behind the counter, diving in to the madness of the harvest festival.

She greeted a young couple mooning over each other and poured them some chardonnay to start. The same gossip and curious glances she had confronted in Lily's filtered through the group to her. Battling to disregard them, she focused instead on the customers before her.

"This is our next chardonnay. It carries a tinge of oak and a buttery flavor," she explained, portioning the correct amount into each glass.

Turning away to allow them to savor the wine, she bumped into Jake.

"I apologize for not arriving sooner. There was something I had to take care of," he said, steadying her.

Her heart soared. "You made it."

He caught her chin for a brief minute. "Of course I did. Your mom said you could show me the ropes around here."

"All right. Let me tell you what we're serving today."

He leaned over to whisper in ear, "I'm sorry about the press. We can talk about it later."

She hadn't decided if she wanted to discuss it or not. Her current plan of ignoring it seemed to be suiting her fine.

"We're offering a red and white flight. The red flight consists of two cabernet sauvignons, a syrah, and a pinot noir. The white flight has two chardonnays and two sauvignon blancs." She spoke at a rapid pace, in full work mode, indicating the different vintages as she went. "We keep the glasses on this shelf."

"What do you think of the new glasses?" he asked, pinching the stem of one for her to observe.

She hadn't noticed that the Oak Hills insignia had been printed on the glassware. Her dad had wanted to do that for a while but hadn't had the available funds. It meant more than it should have to see this small goal of his reached with Jake's assistance.

"They're perfect."

He set the glass down and clapped his hands together. "Let's get this show on the road."

Without a single question, he plunged in and started serving guests with his usual competence and ease, leaving her stunned as she watched him schmooze, tease, and joke with the tourists.

She kept an eye on him while directing her own customers. He charmed the best of them, giving insightful details about the wine she didn't even comprehend and outselling her two to one.

When had he learned so much about her father's wine? The man's potential appeared limitless, missing only a focused course to make him unstoppable.

Adam caught her eye and indicated Jake, giving her a thumbs-up sign. Jake's talent was obvious.

She nodded in agreement.

As she began another tasting, a couple of young women sidled up to Jake's side of the bar, their movements tipsy. She noted their flirtatious smiles and the way the blonde stroked his arm. "Would this cab be better aged or should it be enjoyed now?" a burly man alongside his wife asked.

"You could age it for a couple of years to get a softer taste," she explained. She glanced at the girls again, tipping their heads back with giggles. Jake untangled himself from the blonde as he poured them a significantly smaller portion than what Oak Hills usually served.

She dispensed the sampling of syrah to the couple, glancing over at the little group every two seconds.

"Maybe you could show us around all the local spots," the brunette purred, sliding a finger up Jake's shoulder.

He leaned away from the counter, but that didn't halt the raging stream of jealousy gushing through her.

"Which do you sell more of, the cab or the syrah?" the man questioned, but his voice sounded so far off, she couldn't process it.

She drummed her fingers on the bar.

"Excuse me? Excuse me?"

She turned to her customers. "What? Oh. The cab tends to be more popular."

"I told you, sweetcakes," he said, clinking his glass with his wife's.

Suddenly, the brunette caught her stare.

"Hey, didn't I see your picture in the paper this morning with that gal over there?" the woman asked Jake.

"Oh, say it isn't so. You can't be taken," the blonde pouted, almost falling over the counter onto Jake.

"That's it," Madison mumbled under her breath.

"I think we'll take two bottles of the … "

"Pardon me," she interrupted her customer.

Sauntering over to Jake, she curled into him, resting a possessive hand on his chest. "That's right, ladies, he's mine. So keep off."

Gripping his shirt, she kissed him, not caring what anyone else thought, her single goal being to stake her claim.

Jake pressed her against him, turning up the heat on what she had intended to be a tame kiss. But like everything else about him, his kiss was uncontrollable and she had no intention of suppressing it.

Whoops and cheers sounded throughout the room, and over her shoulder she heard Adam saying something about his eyes burning. None of it held a bearing on her. Not the noises, not the coy girls, and not the paper. Who cared about some article? She had what she cared about in her arms and as long as he was here, she wouldn't let go for anything.

• • •

Once the tasting room was closed and everything cleaned up, her family headed to the house for dinner, but she lingered behind to talk to Jake for a moment alone. A cool night breeze whispered around her, chilling her skin now that the sun had dipped behind the mountains.

She looked down at the ground and waited, not sure where to start.

"I enjoyed seeing your possessive side earlier. You can kiss me like that anytime."

She smiled. "Sounds like a good plan to me."

His expression sobered. "I apologize for the media attention. You mean much more to me than what the paper mentioned. Much more."

"You don't control the press. Besides," she inched closer to him, linking her arms around his neck, "you're worth the price."

He held her tightly, setting his forehead against hers. "You're beyond it. I want to go out with you again. Scratch that, I need to."

She giggled. "That would be wonderful. I don't see how we can manage it, though, with the harvest dinner in a couple of nights."

"We'll figure something out. And afterward, I'd like to take you on our own adventure. Not for the winery, for us."

"Let me guess, it's a surprise?"

He chuckled. "You know me too well. Will you?"

She didn't hesitate. "Yes."

For once, she loved the mystery.

# CHAPTER THIRTEEN

Madison threw back the last dregs of her cold coffee as she stared at the image of her and Jake kissing in the tasting room on the front page of today's paper. She rested her elbow on her shabby desk in her office and set her chin on her fist.

How had they caught them in the act? The photographer must have been hanging out in the tasting room waiting for the perfect moment to pounce. The shot looked cheap. She could have done the special moment justice.

She scrutinized the grainy photo. Still, despite its flaws, it couldn't mask the sense of sweet bliss around them or the romance igniting between them.

She didn't care anymore that their kiss had made the front page. Why wouldn't it? It was tender, loving, and incredible.

The photograph was proof of what her heart already knew. She was half in love with Jake. And how did that mesh with a no-strings-attached relationship with a guy who had no interest in setting down roots? Not well.

A few words on the page caught her eye and she read further down. The article asked if their very own Madison Carmichael could be the one to tame Jake Colt's heart since the reporter received quite the tongue lashing from Jake for her previous story on them.

She reread the same paragraph over and over, drinking in the unbelievable, satisfying words.

He had defended her. Could she claim his heart? Turn this thing between them into something longer lasting?

Could she convince him to stay? She understood what it would mean for him, what he would be giving up in the big city, but she couldn't imagine living anywhere other than Serenity Creek. Her family, her business, her very existence resided here.

And business was picking up. A lot. She had received three more calls this morning alone from brides wanting to meet with her about shooting their weddings. At first she was convinced the additional work had to be related to her newfound notoriety, but her potential clients said it was because of the Oak Hills website, brochures, and other marketing materials Jake had been distributing with her name on it as the photographer.

She set aside the paper and opened up her laptop until the jingle of bells on her door caught her attention. Jake strode in carrying a cardboard tray of iced lattes and a large bag.

"Hey, sweetheart," he greeted. "Lunch?"

"This is a nice surprise." She walked up to him, standing on tiptoe to kiss him.

"Excellent way to say hello. I brought you coffee, but I see you already have some." He indicated the mug on her desk with the tray in his hand.

"That's empty and my cheap stuff. You have the good stuff from Lily's."

She took the tray and bag from him, setting them on the miniscule bistro table and grabbing one of the to-go cups.

"What's for lunch?" she asked.

"Your mom made it for us." He pulled plastic containers out of the bag. "We have tomato and mozzarella sandwiches, potato salad, and brownies."

"Sounds scrumptious." She took a seat, helping arrange their meal.

He sat down across from her.

She bit into her sandwich. "I saw the paper today."

He grunted. "I didn't even want to look."

"You should. It says some good things about you, in my mind at least. Did you really call the reporter and yell at her regarding yesterday's article?"

"No. I went to her office and yelled at her in person. That's why I was late yesterday to the winery. I didn't want you portrayed as just another girl because you're not."

Glad he recognized that because Tucker sure hadn't thought that way.

She settled a hand over her chest. "I can't even tell you how much I appreciate what you did."

He grinned. "Does that mean I'm not just another guy to you?"

"You never were." She laughed, tasting the potato salad. "I'm surprised Mom let you escape to have lunch with me. The winery must be busting at the seams with activity. I'm glad she did, though, really glad."

"She made me leave. I'm sure she knew I wanted to so she packed up lunch and ordered me off the property."

"At least you listen to her when she tells you to leave."

He winked. "I always listen with the correct incentive."

"It's obvious how much my mom wants us to be together."

"That's good, but what's really important is that *you* want us to be together."

"I was going to say the same thing about you."

He widened his eyes. "I thought my going to the reporter and calling her out left no doubt about my intentions."

Were his intentions serious enough for him to make a permanent move, though? The question tickled her tongue, but fear held her back. What if he said no? She didn't understand enough about what he felt for her yet to ask him.

"No, I guess they don't," she said.

She never lied, but she needed time to get a better sense of where things stood between them.

"You did a phenomenal job with those marketing pictures."

"Thanks."

His praise lit her up inside.

"How are things going with my dad? Have you been able to work with him a little or has my mom kidnapped you entirely?"

"Your mom hasn't kidnapped me. There's just been a lot to get done for the harvest dinner. I've spent some time with your dad, though. We've come up with a couple of ideas for some blended wines to try."

"Consider it a compliment. He's pretty strict on whose advice he takes when it comes to his wines."

He shrugged. "It's not my advice. He's been teaching me. I mentioned to him a wine I liked that happened to be a blend of a couple of vintages. I read up on blending, and your dad said he liked the suggestion."

"Uh-huh."

"It's true."

She shrugged. "Sure, whatever you say."

He checked his watch. "I hate to do this, but I have to go. There's still a long list of things to get done before the dinner. I'll pick you up tonight?"

She got to her feet, wrapping her arms around his neck. "Of course. I can't wait."

He nestled her against him. "Neither can I."

He kissed her, running his fingers up her back, leaving a tingling trail in their wake.

• • •

Madison heard the knock resounding through her apartment as she slipped into her red high heels. Grabbing her purse, she rushed to the door, a giddy eagerness fueling her steps.

She opened the door to Jake leaning against the side of the building in his elegant black suit with an open jacket and no tie.

"Hey, sweetheart. Ready to go?"

She nodded. "Definitely."

He tucked her hair behind her ear, kissing her lips before she turned to lock up.

She scanned the parking lot as they descended the stairs, noting a certain car missing.

"Where's the Range Rover?"

He grinned. "I brought a different car today. It's part of the surprise."

Weaving his fingers through hers, he led her to a brand new red Toyota.

She raised her eyebrows.

"This is a bit of a change for you."

He dangled the keys in front of her. "It's yours."

"Mine?"

"Yours."

Shock froze her. She opened and closed her mouth, speechless.

He patted the trunk. "It's nothing fancy. You wouldn't be comfortable in an ostentatious car. But it's new and it's reliable, which is more than I can say for your current mode of transportation."

He had a point and the fact that he comprehended her taste so well made her smile in return, but the gift was way over the top. She might need a car, but she could buy her own. Eventually.

She shook her head. "Thank you. I can't accept it, though."

He pulled her into his arms. "Please. I want you safe and your present car isn't. I want you to have this."

She saw the desperate plea in his eyes for her to take it. Who could resist such a look? And such an offer from a gorgeous, well-meaning man? Receiving help from him might not be so bad.

"It's too much." She gnawed her lower lip.

"So are you, but I would never turn you away. You can't have too much of a good thing. Besides, it's not like I can return it. It lost value just driving it over here."

The man could reason with the best of them and, deep down, she wanted to accept it. Her tiny car held on to life by a thread, and he hadn't bought her something to flash around his money; he had bought her something to keep her safe, something she would like. Maybe he was right. Maybe everyone did need help now and then. Perhaps, it wouldn't be a sign of weakness to accept his assistance.

"All right." She stood on tiptoe to kiss him. "For now. It's unimaginably sweet of you. I can't believe you bought me a car."

A boyish grin spread across his lips, lighting up his face, and she knew she had made the right decision.

"I like taking care of you. Should we go?"

"Sure."

"You get to drive this time." He dropped the keys in her hands.

She climbed into the car, her car.

"Wonders never cease. Next thing you know, you'll be moving to Serenity Creek." She snuck a peek at his face to gauge his reaction.

He had a distinct deer in the headlight look about him. "I don't know what to say to that."

She laughed. "It was just a joke."

Kind of.

Somehow, she had to convince Jake he belonged here with her.

. . .

Jake leaned against the massive, gnarled oak tree behind the Oak Hills winery, observing the last minute bustle of preparations as the catering staff put the final touches in place. He spotted Rose in a long, white dress at the bar they had set up to the side, reviewing a detailed list of descriptions for the wines made available for tonight's dinner. Madison, in her gorgeous red gown and massive curls pulled over to one side, stood beside her. He had pulled it together. With massive amounts of help from Rose and Thomas, but he had done it. He had ensured all the pieces were in place for a successful night and had turned the marketing blitz with the sweepstakes into some very profitable business for the winery.

Thomas had even told Jake that he had a knack for being a vintner.

He smiled. Wouldn't that be something? Him as a winemaker.

They had taken him in, treated him as if he belonged there with them, something his father had never even done. It gave him an anchor, focused his thoughts. He had learned what mattered most in life.

What he had done for the winery, he did with his own two hands. It hadn't been given to him; he had worked for it, and he found the sensation irresistible, like the woman who had been his motivation through it all.

Maybe Madison had been right in the car. She'd caught him off guard with her comment about moving, but it might not be so outlandish after all.

As guests arrived, he pushed off from the tree and put on his best networking face, ready to do some serious schmoozing. He shook hands, told the right jokes, said the perfect words, and worked the crowd until his phone buzzed in his pocket.

He ignored it, moving along his conversation with the head of the local vintner's association, but a call came through a second time. Then a third.

Sliding his phone out, he peeked at the caller ID and groaned under his breath.

Holding up a finger he said, "Excuse me, please. I have to take this."

Three calls in a row from his father usually didn't carry great news.

His gut clenched as he walked to a lantern-strewn tree on the sideline of the event.

"Yes, Clayton," he answered, keeping any sense of foreboding out of his voice.

"I saw the numbers for the winery. Things are looking good there."

"That's right. Can we talk about this later? I'm in the middle of the harvest dinner."

"Who cares about some bumpkin celebration? And no, we can't talk about this later. Seems you've been busy with more than just the winery, according to the tabloids."

He noted the accusation in his father's tone.

"And your point is?" Jake sighed.

"Don't get attached to a job that's over and done with."

"I don't expect you to understand anything about attachment or feelings, but I do expect you to … " He broke off as Clayton's words clicked. "Wait, what do you mean over and done with?"

"I mean your work there is done. You held up your end of our agreement and started turning things around with the winery. Now, it's time to kick things into overdrive there and get rid of the property to make room for something more profitable. And you need to get back to the office so we can decide on your next project."

Jake curled his fingers into a fist, cursing under his breath. A sickening sensation slithered through his stomach.

"There's no 'we' in this decision. I get to choose my new assignment, and I choose the Carmichael winery as it is, no changes necessary."

"That's not an option," Clayton growled, his voice as strong and cold as granite. "I've already set the wheels in motion to start demolishing the place."

"That's never been part of my plan."

"But it's always been a part of mine. It's the same with all of our properties and well you know it."

"We agreed to do things my way, this time." Jake ground his teeth.

"You agreed. And we did do things your way at first. But knocking down the place to make room for a larger operation was arranged from the start. We'll set up a substantial hotel and restaurant. Get rid of the grapes all together. I already have some chains interested."

"You can't do this, Clayton."

Clayton chuckled. "Oh, I can, son, and I have. Come on, you don't want to be there, anyway. Come back here and take your pick of where you want to go. Australia, France, China."

His heart pounded. "And if I choose to leave the company entirely, then what?"

"You wouldn't dare."

"And if I did?"

"You'd be walking away from everything. I'll disown you so fast your head will spin."

Jake clenched his fist. "Just like that?"

"What's gotten into your head? It can't possibly have anything to do with this girl, could it? Not exactly the type of girl you want to align yourself with." Clayton's sarcasm drenched the phone line.

"You don't know anything about her."

Jake scanned the crowd, searching for Madison. He spotted her in the distance laughing with her brother, her blonde curls dipping down her back and pure delight radiating from her. He wanted to be next to her, to be the cause of her happiness. His father had never been more wrong.

"I don't need to. I'll give you until the end of the day tomorrow to make your decision and get your butt back here where it belongs."

The dead sound ringing in his ear indicated that this time around Clayton had hung up on him.

He ran through the options in his mind at lightning speed. It would kill Madison to see her family and their winery torn apart to make way for some large chain hotel. He couldn't leave her.

But if his father disowned him, Jake would lose the only family he had left, sad as it was, and what he would do with his life? He couldn't very well run the winery with Thomas if it was annihilated to make room for some large operation.

Threads of an idea began to form in the back of his head. If he could make the right pieces fall into place, he might be able to pull something off, but it was a long shot, laden with risks.

He watched Madison and her brother toasting near the tables, Thomas and Rose exchanging a quick kiss under the trees, and guests milling about the outdoor tasting area. They were fragments of a life too treasured to let go of. He had to protect them.

He wouldn't tell Madison about the pending demolition or his sole idea to get them out of this mess. Not yet. Not until he knew he had a chance of winning. He didn't want her to worry about something he might be able to take care of without her ever being wise to just how devious and conniving his father could be. And if he couldn't do it, the winery would be sold, she'd blame him, and she'd be right as she walked out on him.

The key was to move fast. He had to get the ball rolling. Anything to keep him from envisioning his life without Madison.

Using his cell phone, he made arrangements to be on the first available flight to New York. He'd take his MD 600N to LAX. His contacts were centered in New York. He'd handle as much as he could from the plane.

Never had he been so desperate for one of his plans to succeed.

His heart plummeted as he confirmed his travel arrangements. He had to make Madison understand his departure, but he didn't have time for a lengthy explanation, especially in the middle of the party. His taxi would be here any minute, and he barely had enough time to make it to LAX to catch his flight. He'd have to fill her in once he arrived.

Striding up to her in the crowd, he slipped his arm around her waist and leaned next to her ear to whisper, "Something's come up. I have to go. I'll call you later."

Her eyebrows furrowed. "Is everything okay? Do you need me to go with you?"

"No, you stay. I've already arranged a cab." He kissed her cheek. "Enjoy the night."

He walked out of the feast, strains of music fading into the darkness behind him. He prayed he could make this work and save Oak Hills and Madison, because the alternative was unimaginable and turned his blood cold.

# CHAPTER FOURTEEN

Madison walked the new bride she had just signed a contract with to the door.

"It was a pleasure meeting with you, Trixie, and I look forward to discussing specific shots with you." She pulled open the door for her.

"Thank you, Madison. I'll see you soon." Trixie walked out of her office into the fading evening sun.

Madison closed the door behind her with a rush of excitement. Her last client gone and she hoped to chat with Jake soon. She had everything planned out on how to persuade him they could build a life together in Serenity Creek, complete with her family's photo album with some embarrassing shots of herself growing up to show him later as a last resort.

She strode back to her desk, checking her phone again for a call from Jake. He'd left her a brief message last night while she had been finishing up at the party, but every time she tried calling him today it ended up going to voicemail, and her day had been packed with back-to-back appointments.

She listened to his earlier message once more, the words echoing down to her heart.

He had to go to New York on urgent business and didn't have time to stay for the event and explain as he wanted to. He would miss his flight if he experienced even a five-minute delay. He would miss her and they'd talk soon.

She kept repeating his speech over and over in her head in an attempt to drown out the nagging concern ringing in her ears. He had left. It sounded like he hadn't wanted to, but he had all the same. After her comment about him moving to Serenity Creek. Just like Tucker.

Her hands trembled despite her best efforts to remain calm. What could be so important that he had to take off so fast?

Her phone jingled and she almost dropped it in her rush to answer.

"Jake?"

"Sorry, no. It's Adam."

His grave tone startled her, such a stark contrast from his usual jovial attitude.

"Oh, of course. What's up?"

"You need to meet me at mom and dad's ASAP."

Her pulse quickened, her tummy rolling. "Why? What's the matter?"

"I don't know all of the details. Just get there. Fast."

She tightened her grip on her phone to keep it from quaking. "I'm on my way."

Her heart pounded as she dumped all of her things into her satchel, grabbed her laptop, and locked up her office.

She climbed into her car, throwing her things on the passenger seat. The car Jake had given her. When would he be back?

Shaking her head, she shoved the key in the ignition and took off for her parents' place. Her family needed her now. She couldn't dwell on her own worries if she was going to help them with whatever had occurred.

She sped through town, grateful for a working car she didn't have to turn over multiple times to get it to start.

A thousand thoughts ran through her mind. Different scenarios for what trouble her parents could be in. What if her dad had had a heart attack? What if someone in their family had died?

Adam's call on top of Jake's message left her reeling. She had trouble focusing on the road.

Taking a long, slow breath, she negotiated the roads to the winery with extra care. She would be of no aid to her parents if she arrived a bundle of nerves.

As she parked in front of her parent's house, she noted Adam's car under one of the oak trees.

Squaring her shoulders, she shoved down her anxiousness over Jake, and stepped through the front door.

"Hello?" she called out.

"In the kitchen," Rose answered.

She made her way to the back of the house and into the kitchen where she saw her parents at the breakfast table and Adam pacing before them. Everyone turned to her, their expressions dire.

She stopped at the center island. "What happened? What's wrong?"

Thomas rested his elbows on his knees, leaning forward. "We received a call from Clayton Colt an hour ago. He sold Oak Hills. The deal's new and the details are still being worked out so we don't know who the new owner is or what the terms are, but Colt Enterprises is out."

Everything spun around her in an ugly mess of colors. She gripped the counter to steady herself, but nothing could calm the storm raging through her.

That's why Jake bolted town so quickly. He had finished his job and couldn't wait to leave, not even to face her and tell her about the sale in person. Not even to say goodbye. He must have known what his father had planned. He was a VP in the company for crying out loud. Why hadn't he told her?

Because she would have moved heaven and earth to stop it, anything to save her parents and he knew it.

He had betrayed her more than Tucker ever had.

Had he ever loved her? Or had he just said it to placate her, to distract her from what Clayton was organizing behind the scenes? Had any of their relationship been real?

Nausea threatened her as she fought to think straight.

"Maddy, are you all right?" Adam clasped her shoulders, staring her straight in the eye.

She blinked at him, nodding. "Yes. I'm fine. We'll get through this. Somehow. As a family."

She spoke the words but inside she felt dead. Sure, they could repair their lives, weave some semblance of normalcy back into their existence. She had before and she could now. It would never be the same, though. Not only had Jake deceived her, he had deceived her family and that was unforgivable.

She looked past Adam to her parents, their brokenness evident in their slumped frames and the tiny tear trickling down her mom's cheek. No one knew who the new owner could be and that meant they had no clue what the sale of Oak Hills, their lifeblood, would mean to them and their way of living. Would her parents even still be a part of it? Would they continue to live in the same house they had been in for decades?

She clenched her hands tightly, guarding her tongue until she could lock down the anger and hurt raging within her. She had to support her parents, comfort them in any way she could. Later, much later, she'd work to heal the wounds left in the wake of Jake's lies.

• • •

Jake stared his father down across the massive desk that had been in their family for generations. He hated that piece of furniture as much as he did the rest of Clayton's office and the Colt building. He couldn't wait to wipe that smug smile off Clayton's face.

Clayton leaned forward, resting his forearms on his desk. "Well, I'm glad you've seen reason and decided to come home. I always knew you would."

Jake clenched his jaw to keep from saying the wrong thing. "I'm not back. Yet."

"What are you talking about?" Clayton scowled.

"I'm here to ask for an extension. I need time to think this through."

Clayton responded in the exact way he had expected.

"Think it through? There's nothing to think through. The decision is simple. Your place is here. So what's it going to be, boy? Which assignment do you want? Hong Kong? Paris?"

"You'd really demolish the winery, tear apart the Carmichael family, just to turn a profit?"

Clayton shrugged. "We're a business, that's what we do. Make money. There's nothing wrong with that."

"It's a matter of how you go about it."

"You're right, you choose the path with the highest return."

"So let me handle the Oak Hills project. See it through to make sure you get the best deal."

Clayton huffed. "I don't need your help negotiating and that project's over and done with. Not an option for you. In fact, speaking of higher returns, I'm just about to sign an agreement to sell it. Got an offer sent over a few hours ago. It'll be easier than dealing with the headache of that miniscule piece of land. Now seems like the perfect time so you'll get the silly winery out of your head."

At last. It had taken his father long enough.

He watched as Clayton snatched a thin stack of papers from the corner of his desk. He flipped to the last page and scribbled his stark signature across the bottom.

Jake fought hard to not show the relief washing over him. He was too close to blow it all now.

"So I have to give you an answer now, then?" Jake rubbed his jaw.

Clayton slammed his pen down on the desk. "I'm not playing games anymore. You will pick an acquisition and carry out my legacy under my direction and command."

"No."

Clayton narrowed his eyes. "What did you say?"

Jake stood up. "I said no. I'm not going to be your puppet. I never have been and I never will. I'm leaving. I want to build my own life, separate from Colt Enterprises."

"If you think I'll back down, you're dead wrong. My attorney will be the next call I make to cut you out of everything. Do you really think your little gold digger will stick around after her parents' winery is sold and you don't have a cent to your name?" Clayton picked up the phone.

Jake curled his fingers into the palm of his hands, anything to keep from losing his cool. "I don't need your money; neither of us do. You can make your decision. I've made mine."

Jake turned to leave.

"Don't you turn your back on me, boy. A Colt has run this company since my grandfather founded it. You'll be back," Clayton shouted.

Jake walked out of the office without looking back. He grinned as he shut the door behind him, drowning out Clayton's tirade. Everything was falling into place.

• • •

Madison curled deeper into the sage throw blanket tucked around her on her couch, letting her tears slip down her cheeks one by one. Sipping the chardonnay she had poured herself and munching on her second brownie, she stared blankly ahead through the dampness blurring her eyesight.

The brownies had been a must and she had picked them up on her way home. The whole town already knew of the sale, including the clerk behind the counter of the grocery store who had given her the saddest, most pitying look she'd ever seen. The speed with which gossip traveled in Serenity Creek had always irritated her, never more than in that moment. Jake had had a point there, but that didn't matter now. She hadn't made it to her car before Tessa had called her, offering to meet her at her apartment. For once, she had turned Tessa down. She needed to be alone to wallow and think.

How could he have betrayed her so? She thought he had changed, had gained some direction and responsibility. But he couldn't even be counted on to own up to his actions in person. He fled rather than face her with the truth of what he had done.

The ugly truth smothered her. He had never cared about her. He had used their dates, his mumblings of affection to distract her from the winery and what Colt Enterprises had going on behind their backs.

She didn't want to believe him capable of such evil, didn't want to admit everything between them had been false. The pieces only fit together one way, though, and they painted a cruel picture.

Perhaps, he had been interested in her. After all, his intentions appeared clear from the beginning, but love constituted another matter entirely. Could a playboy like him really love one woman?

It seemed a stretch to believe now when she wasn't under his hypnotic spell. His using sentiment as a means to accomplish his own ends jarred much more with reality.

And yet, she still couldn't deny the tenderness of his touch, the sweet sensation of his lips on hers.

Her phone rang. She groaned. Not another person seeking out information about the sale and where Jake had gone. The whole town had been calling her.

She checked her caller ID and the name on the screen set her every nerve on alert. Her stomach flipped as she shoved her hand against her cheek, wiping away her tears.

Part of her wanted to ignore Jake. Another part of her, though, a stronger part, desired nothing more than to lay into him for his misdeeds.

"Hello, Jake," she answered, her tone level and cool.

She heard his low chuckle. The jerk.

"Sweetheart, you have no idea how good it is to hear your voice. I have so much to tell you."

His calm, almost joyful words, grated on her bruised soul. He was acting like nothing had happened.

"I just bet you do. Why don't you start with how you sold us out and skipped town so fast you didn't even have the decency to say goodbye and stick around to see the fallout of your and your father's actions?"

Her whole body tensed as if preparing for battle.

"What are you talking about?"

The dam holding her emotions back broke. "I'm talking about Colt Enterprises selling my parents' winery, as if you didn't know. I'm talking about you using me, lying to keep me focused on you and not what your father had planned for Oak Hills. I'm talking about you not even being capable of telling me to my face what you did, what your father did, you inconsiderate, backstabbing liar."

She gulped in a few quick breaths to try to calm herself. As if that were possible.

"It's not what you think. You have to listen to me."

"Why? To hear you spin more tales? To let you break my heart all over again?"

"To hear the truth." A hard edge crept into his tone. "You're awfully quick to pass judgment on someone. I thought you trusted me."

"That was before you lied to me."

"I never lied to you."

She hit the pillow with her fist, anger humming through her. "No, you just conveniently left out some details, like the fact that you were making arrangements to sell Oak Hills, or your father was and you turned a blind eye. Either way, you omitted some pretty important facts, don't you think?"

"Have I kept things from you? Yes. And that's what really upsets you in all of this, isn't it? More than the fact the winery was sold, it's that you didn't know about it. Never mind my side of the story or the fact that I have good reasons for not having told you everything. For once, you didn't have full control of your perfect world." He spat the words out like a curse.

"I haven't had control since you landed here."

"Madison." He sighed, his voice softer. "I have a plan and it's already been set in motion."

She squeezed her eyes shut, her throat clogged and burning. "I bet it has. I'm not buying any more of your ideas. You're in New York where you wanted to be and where you belong. You're just like your father. Don't call me anymore. Goodbye, Jake."

She threw the phone on the other side of the couch, drawing her knees up to her chest and resting her head against them. She found herself in the exact spot she had promised herself she wouldn't be again, only this time the loss was greater and the hurt deeper.

Sobs shook her body as tears wet the blanket. His accusation of what truly upset her had hit its mark. But so what? He should have been upfront with her. The only reason to hide anything would be guilt, and he reeked of it. And, of course, she was livid over the actual sale itself. Who wouldn't be?

*I have a plan and it's already been set in motion.*

She couldn't begin to know if he did or not or if it would hurt or help them, but his words gave rise to a dangerous flicker of hope. She dare not stoke its flames. Hope held too much uncertainty. It could save her or set her up to fail and fall victim to more of Jake's tall tales. And yet, it stirred her heart, beckoning her to believe.

# CHAPTER FIFTEEN

Jake lowered his cell phone, the blood in his veins turning to ice. He stared head on into the harsh reality before him. He had lost Madison. And not because his plan had failed. All the parts of his strategy were coming together. But because she wouldn't hear him out, wouldn't give him a chance to explain that whatever lies Clayton had infected the Carmichaels with were just that, lies.

He hadn't expected his father to tell them about the deal so fast. Considering the timing, he must have called them before he even signed the paperwork. It shouldn't have surprised him. To Clayton, the deal had been completed when he received the offer he would have been a fool to turn down, his signature being a formality. Still, his father couldn't have told them the truth since Clayton didn't even know the whole story. Only he did.

Maybe he had been wrong in not telling Madison his idea from the start of this whole mess, but he had been trying to protect her and help her family. He hadn't meant to lose his temper with her. He shouldn't have. Except that he'd been working at a grueling pace to fix things since that despicable call with his father and it had all been for nothing, since she wouldn't even pay attention to him.

Control. He was so sick of it. His father obsessed over it and Madison needed it. And he needed her.

He walked over to the mirrored glass bar off to the side of his living room, and poured himself a shot of whiskey. The night had called for celebration, not facing the fact that every passing minute Madison slipped further through his fingers and out of his grasp.

Her words ricocheted through him, each one like the sound of a gunshot. *To let you break my heart again.* He tightened his grip on the glass until he thought it might break. He never wanted to hurt her. Everything he was doing was to protect her. 'You're just like your father'. Her remark burned a trail down his throat along with the whiskey, straight to his gut, scorching everything inside him. No statement could have been worse to hear, especially from her.

He threw back the rest of the drink, scanning the room to take in the cold, austere environment that made up his New York penthouse. The place stood devoid of any warmth. No pictures, no family antiques, no signs of life besides the sparse furnishings and skyline view. Nothing like Madison's apartment or her family's home where every inch welcomed you, beckoning you to stay.

He missed that familiarity. He missed them. And more than anything, he ached to hold Madison. To kiss her and tell her everything would be all right, he had it all taken care of. To tell her he'd give up anything to be with her, including a big city life and the only family he'd ever known, the company his ancestors had started generations ago. Because what mattered most had became obvious the minute Clayton had threatened him.

Being in New York lacked the same appeal, the same rush it usually gave him. Instead, he kept dreaming of open vineyards covered in sunlight and quiet, cool nights with Madison nestled next to him.

He set his empty glass on the bar, striding over to the floor-to-ceiling windows to watch the cars buzzing past on the streets below while pedestrians milled about the sidewalk. Lights blazed everywhere, and down there was a sea of people, yet he had never felt more alone.

He'd done it. He'd broken things off with his father. Only a few things remained to get done to finalize his grand design. All to save the Carmichaels and their winery and keep Madison in his life. Yet, he had still lost her. Because she refused to see the truth in the matter. Not that he could blame her. Clayton was a mastermind of deceit. Still, her rejection stung like a freezing winter wind on the Alps.

Money had always gotten him out of any problem, but not this time. No amount of money would bring Madison back to him.

Rubbing the back of his neck, he ran through the situation in his mind. He would not admit defeat. She mattered more to him than anything else and he would not let her go without a fight.

As the numbness in his body eased, the path cleared before him. He'd tie up the loose strings left with his contacts to rescue Oak Hills and make a final commitment to Madison, hopefully one she couldn't turn down.

• • •

The bright morning sun contrasted with the gloom surrounding Madison as she walked into Lily's coffeehouse. Try as she might, no amount of cover-up could hide the dark circles under her puffy eyes, and she didn't care anymore. She had spent the night wide awake, staring at her ceiling, going over her conversation with Jake until she had questioned every little nuance of what he had said.

By the wee dawn hours, a horrible inkling that she should have given him at least a chance to explain, that maybe she was missing something in all of this, had taken root in her. But she still couldn't bring herself to pick up the phone and call him. Too many variables existed, including her parents and her loyalty to them. Would she be betraying them to confer with the enemy?

She tucked her head down, hiding from the curious onlookers in the coffee shop and made her way straight to the counter.

"Hey, Lily. Can I please get a large latte? Double shot."

"Madison, how are you holding up?" Lily asked, genuine sympathy shining in her gaze.

"I don't want to talk about it," Madison mumbled.

Lily lowered her gaze. "I understand. Pretty bad, huh? I'll get your order right away."

Madison's outlook sank even lower as Lily busied herself with the coffee. She hadn't meant to be rude. She just didn't want to discuss everything with the morning crowd eavesdropping.

"Here you are. This one's on the house." Lily set a steaming to-go cup in front of her.

"Thanks, Lily. You have to stop giving me free stuff or I could get used to it."

Lily laughed, a soft sound. "You've been a loyal customer for a long time, and I always like to help a friend in need in any way I can. Even if it's just coffee."

"I appreciate it."

Madison waved on her way out the door, making a mental note that once her life had some semblance of order again she should do something for Lily to properly thank her for her support.

With her latte in hand, she walked over to The Wine Cork. She had too many questions, ideas, and notions running rampant in her head. She needed someone to dump them on. Someone to help her sort them out.

Breathing in the rich scent of fresh roasted coffee beans, she took a deep sip of the strong drink, reveling in the kick-start it blasted through her. At least it gave her enough energy to make it to Adam's.

She went in through the back knowing the front door would be closed until they opened for lunch.

She ignored the concerned glances from the workers she passed. If she dwelt on them, she would burst into tears again and that wouldn't do in a public place.

Poking her head into Adam's office, she spotted him hunched over his desk reviewing paperwork. He looked up at her knock. He didn't appear much better than her with his unshaven face and rumpled hair. She understood his worry over their parents all too well.

"Do you have a minute?" she asked.

"Of course. Have a seat." He indicated the chair opposite his desk.

She sat down, cradling her cup in her hands. She spotted Adam's longing stare in the direction of her coffee.

"Would you like some?" she offered.

He shook his head. "No, no. I'm good." He tipped his mug toward him and frowned. "I'll make some more coffee later."

She shrugged. "All right."

"How are you doing?"

She gave a deep sigh that seemed to reach to the farthest caverns of her heart. "Same as you apparently. I'm worried about mom and dad."

He leveled her with his disbelieving eyes. "You're worried about a lot more than that."

She nodded, nibbling her lip. "Yeah."

"You're worried about Jake."

"Yeah," she said. The single word quivered as tears bunched in her eyes. "I can't believe he would do this to us. He never mentioned anything and then he up and left without so much as a goodbye or an apology for ruining our parents' lives and jerking me around all of this time."

He pushed back in his seat. "I admit things don't look too great for the guy, but he did try to talk to you before he left, right?"

"Yes."

That was the other piece that kept tugging at her to believe him. What if she hadn't missed his call? Would he have told her what was going to happen? Would it have made a difference?

"He called last night, too," she added.

He whistled. "Must have been a fun conversation. What did he say?"

At this point, she could recite every part of it, but she figured her brother would be more interested in the summary.

"He said he missed me, that he has already implemented a plan."

"Like what? That could mean a lot of things."

Guilt drenched her like a cold rain. The realization had struck her last night, the only one to become clear to her. She should have asked him.

"I don't know."

His eyes widened. "He didn't tell you?"

She winced. "I didn't let him."

"I see." He gave her the brotherly look he always did when she did something wrong and he wished he could make it better for her.

"I know, I know. I should have heard him out, but I was in no state to listen to him last night. I couldn't make out if he would tell me the truth or more lies. That's the problem. I don't know what's fact and what's fiction in any of this."

"Only one man does."

"Yeah and it's the one man I don't know if I can trust."

"Yes, you do, Maddy."

His quiet statement sliced through her. She loved Jake and despite everything that had happened, she believed she could trust him, which meant she might have ruined her chance in the way she had treated him.

She rubbed her eyes, remembering the moment she had said he was like his father. From what Jake had told her about his relationship with his father, her statement topped the list as the nastiest words she could have uttered. Not to mention all the other barriers that stood between them.

And then she had her parents to consider. Believing Jake, talking with him seemed in direct conflict to supporting her parents.

"You care about him, don't you?"

A single tear slid down her cheek. "Yes."

He sighed. "I'm not his biggest fan, but if you like him, then I can put up with him a lot better than I could some of your other boyfriends."

She chuckled. Her brother could always make her laugh, no matter what.

"There's too much between us."

"Like what?"

"Let's start with the entire continent. My concept of a relationship is with someone at least on the same coast as I am. You have no idea how mean I was on the phone. And what about Mom and Dad? Jake must have known about the upcoming sale; why didn't he warn us?"

As she spoke her fears out loud, the cloud surrounding her mind began to clear. She could start to see the decision before her and what she had to do. She just had to find the courage to do it.

"Those are questions for Jake, not me. Do you really want to live a life without him?"

The thought pierced her heart like a dagger. It had been the nightmare churning in her head since this whole mess struck her. She couldn't bear to be without him. And yet, she could not, would not betray her parents.

She shook her head, her throat too clogged up to speak.

"Then what are you waiting for? Call him," he said in a gentle tone.

"We've past the calling mark. Something else is required."

He squinted at her. "What do you mean?"

She rose from her chair. "I have to think it through first."

He stood, pointing his finger at her. "I know that look. It means trouble." He came around to give her a tight hug. "Whatever's going on in that brain of yours, though, you know I'm behind you no matter what."

"Thank you," she whispered.

He ruffled her hair. "Go get him."

She pushed his hand away with a giggle and sprinted through the restaurant. Finishing the last of her coffee, she chucked it in the trash on her way out the door.

Her soul had split in half. A part loved Jake with such fierce devotion it would not waver. The other supported her parents with steadfast loyalty. She existed in the center of a tug of war between two opposing sides.

She kept imagining if the situation was reversed and it was her business on the line being sold out from under her. She'd be crushed and she assumed her parents would respond in the same way to the bitter defeat before them.

Doubling back to her car, she settled on her next move. She had to talk to her mom and dad. If she gave in to the crazy scheme forming in her mind, she had to tell them first.

A short drive later, she opened her parents' front door, immersing herself in the scent of chocolate chip cookies.

"Hello?" she called out.

"In the kitchen," Rose answered.

She followed her mother's voice and the delicious smell of baked dough and chocolate.

"Hey, Mom." She enveloped her mother in her arms.

Rose patted her back. "Now, now, dear. Have a seat."

Rose pointed at the kitchen table.

Madison slid into a chair as Rose placed a fresh cup of coffee and a plate of cookies in front of her.

Madison laughed. "How did you know I was coming?"

Rose smiled. "Mother's intuition. Adam confirmed my suspicion a little bit ago when he called to say you might be coming over."

Her family knew her too well and she loved them for it.

She sipped the hot coffee. After her sleepless night, she could use all the caffeine she could get her hands on and one would have to be dead to turn down her mother's coffee.

She helped herself to a cookie and bit into the warm, gooey treat, sinking into its sugary delight, a temporary relief from the pain of the past twenty-four hours.

Rose took a seat opposite her. "Want to tell me about it?"

"Jake called me last night."

"You talked to him, then?"

"Not exactly. I hung up on him."

Rose's jaw dropped. "Why? Did he say something awful?"

"No, I didn't give him a chance to say much of anything."

"Oh." Rose nodded. "Why didn't you?"

"Because he lied to me, all of us." Madison threw her arms out wide. "At least he may have. I know I should have heard his side of the story, but I was too angry then to think about it that way."

"And now?"

"And now I'm afraid of betraying you and Dad. Jake's your adversary and talking with him, giving him a chance, feels like going behind your back."

Rose made a tsking sound with her tongue. "Who said Jake was our adversary?" She patted Madison's hand. "Sweetie, relationships aren't always easy. Sometimes it requires hard choices and brutal battles, but you triumph over the bad with the strength and courage the other person gives you."

The tension in her chest released its grasp a little. Perhaps her parents would approve after all.

"But look at what he did to you guys."

Rose shrugged. "Who knows what his part in all of this really is. Maybe he's as innocent as the rest of us. Why would he build up the winery only to sell it?"

She had thought of that too. "To fetch a better price."

"Do you believe Jake capable of something so manipulative?"

She answered with her heart. "No."

"At the end of the day, the winery is just that, a winery. It's a thing. What matters most to me is your father and you two kids. As long as I have you three, that's all I need."

Thomas strode in through the back door. "Me, too. Family is the most important asset of a person's life."

He settled an arm around Rose's shoulders, kissing the top of her head. "Think about it this way. If you could have the most thriving photography business in the world but had no one to share your success or happiness with, would it mean anything to you?"

The concept hit her like a slap in the face. Jake had become far more important to her than her photography, which meant their family was more important to her parents than the winery. And nothing could break them apart.

"If I were to … that is, I've been thinking … would you guys … " She trailed off in frustration, not able to figure out how to voice her question aloud.

Thomas sat down next to Madison, placing his hand on her knee. "I know you've come for affirmation from us, I see it in your eyes. But you don't need it. You have to make the choice that's right for you. Your mother and I always have and always will love you."

The truth of his statement nestled deep within her, confirming the decision she had made on the drive over here. The decision that, if she were honest with herself, she had made last night.

"Thanks, Dad." Madison got to her feet and kissed her father's cheek.

She hugged her mother.

"Don't just be loyal to your family, be loyal to your heart." Rose spoke into her ear.

"I will, Mom."

Saying goodbye to her parents, she rushed to her car. A thousand thoughts fluttered through her head of what lay before her. Fear and excitement coursed through her, making it hard to concentrate on the simple task of getting the key into the ignition.

She had so much to do in such a short amount of time. First, she had to pack, then she had a plane to catch. An actual plane. She hoped this city experience would go better than the last.

# CHAPTER SIXTEEN

Madison gripped the armrests of the plane seat until her knuckles ached and she could no longer feel the distinction of where her hands ended and the handles began. The pilot had just announced they would be taxiing soon, which had sent her stomach into a series of manic flips. She had never in her life expected to be on a large plane flying across the country on a spur of the moment decision to fix something where she had no power over the outcome. It rested solely with one man. But then she hadn't anticipated half the curveballs life had thrown her recently.

The plane lurched backwards and she jumped in her seat, squeezing her eyes shut.

"First time flying?" the old lady with a kind appearance that had settled next to her asked.

She peeked out of one eye. "Yes."

Her nerves dangled on a razor sharp edge. She needed Jake's presence to calm her down.

The plane thumped along to the takeoff runway, every thud jolting her heart, before coming to a halt.

"Don't worry, dear, this is the fun part." The old lady patted her arm.

Madison cinched her seatbelt tighter, leaned her head back and shut her eyes again, letting out a long breath.

The plane shot off like a bullet, grinding her into the seat. Sweat drenched her palms, making them slick against the armrests. What had she been thinking when she boarded the giant, uncontrollable sum of all her fears?

She pictured Jake. His handsome, familiar face, the feel of his strong, safe touch, his encouraging words of comfort. She recalled why she was flying to the east coast. For him. To fix things between them, even if it meant living there to be with him.

Her pulse slowed with each thought as the plane tilted off the ground and took to the skies. Once it leveled out so did her tummy and she opened her eyes one at a time.

"Feeling better, now? I'm Claire Merberry," the old lady introduced herself.

Madison shook her hand. "Madison Carmichael."

"What takes you to New York? Business or pleasure?"

More. Much more. "A guy."

Claire cooed. "I adore romantic stories. Are you meeting your fiancé? Flying to see your boyfriend for a passionate getaway?"

"It's a long story."

"It's a long flight. Tell me everything."

Madison squirmed, but she had to talk to someone, and right now Claire was the only person available. She told her about Jake, how they met, working together, falling for him, and her stupid mistake in not trusting him when the cards had been down on the table.

"Love forgives any number of wrongs and doesn't keep track of them. You'll see. It'll be all right. Does he know you're coming?" Claire grinned.

Madison twisted the hem of her floral skirt. "No. I haven't spoken to him since I told him not to call me."

"Why not?"

"I need to see him in person. I can't do this over the phone."

Claire studied her with the knowing look of a woman who had had her share of experience with relationships.

Madison sighed. "And I didn't want to risk him telling me not to come. That it was pointless. I wanted him to understand how much he means to me, that I truly am sorry. I figured flying across the country, which is a big thing for me by the way, could help him see that."

Claire squeezed her shoulder. "As I said, it'll be all right. My Roland and I, we've had a few spouts over our forty plus years of marriage and I'm sure we're not done, but we keep going and making up is the best part." Claire winked at her.

Madison smiled, picturing the expression on Jake's face when he saw her, praying he would forgive her and that he had nothing to do with the sale of Oak Hills.

She spent the rest of the flight chatting with Claire, finding out about her marriage to her high school sweetheart and their three grown children, about the grandkids she was flying out to babysit while her daughter and son-in-law took a Caribbean cruise. All the while, her mind rested on Jake. She wanted that life with him, whether it be in Serenity Creek, New York, or somewhere else. She couldn't stop thinking about him, about what she should say to him when she arrived.

The flight went faster than she thought it would and before she knew it they had touched down in New York. Landing had been jarring but as long as she imagined Jake next to her holding her hand she was okay.

Madison helped Claire get her carry-on bag down from the overhead storage bins. She passed the woman her bag and followed her off the plane.

Claire hugged her as they entered the gate waiting area. "Don't worry. Love conquers all, dear, love conquers all."

Madison waved as Claire went on her way.

She had just flown on a plane on her own. She could face Jake, apologize to him, and make him see they had a future together.

Clutching the strap of her miniature duffel bag, the only luggage she had brought with her, she made her way through the hordes of people filling the maze of the large airport.

By following the instructions of numerous signs, she saw daylight and stepped outside into heat and loud noises all around her. Everywhere she turned, people talked on cell phones and sprinted past her, their baggage slamming into her as they swarmed taxicabs.

After so many attempts that she lost count, she managed to grab one for herself and slid into the backseat, her skirt catching on the cracked leather of the seat.

"Where to?" the cabbie asked, his gaze never straying from the front window.

She fumbled in her wallet and then gave him Jake's business card. "Colt Enterprises, please."

After a traffic filled cab ride, Madison stared up at the enormous skyscraper before her surrounded by dozens more just like it. They filled the entire city like a dense, concrete forest. She couldn't believe the number of people that charged through the streets or the deafening cacophony of horns and jackhammers. Everything appeared out of focus to her. Jake lived in all of this, thrived on the rush of it all. Could he ever be happy living a slower pace with her? If not, she'd just have to become accustomed to this new speed of life.

She straightened up, standing to her full height and shifted her bag on her shoulder. Taking a deep breath, she pushed open the massive glass door with Colt Enterprises emblazoned on it.

Black and white marble tile floors spread the length of the lobby, and were flanked on either side by a row of gold door elevators with people cycling through them at a steady pace. Crystal chandeliers dangled from an impossibly high ceiling. No chairs, tables, magazines, or welcome desk could be seen. Everything about the space appeared formal and detached, encouraging workers to get on their way and not linger.

For the first time, Madison felt uncomfortable in her own flat, sensible shoes. She tugged at her skirt and simple top, touched the rumpled bun her hair had become after the long flight, and noticed the increased pressure against her side from her undersized luggage. How could she and Jake come from such different worlds?

But she had to know if they still stood a chance. She'd come this far and she refused to turn back now.

She snagged an elevator to the fifty-second floor, her heart jumping into her throat as the doors slid open.

She stepped onto plush dark green carpet and followed the elaborate sign to Jake's office.

A woman she figured had to be Jake's assistant busied herself with arranging or taking things down off her desk in the large alcove at one end of the hallway. She moved with great efficiency around her space, a single strand of brown hair tinged with gray daring to slip out of her tight bun.

She walked up to the desk. "Excuse me, I'm looking for Jake Colt. Do you know where I might find him?"

The assistant didn't break her pace as she stuffed files into a box. "Not here, that's for sure."

"I guess he doesn't spend much time here, huh? I'm Madison Carmichael." She offered her hand to the assistant.

The woman jammed in her last file and stopped to shake Madison's hand, taking in her appearance from her head to her toes before smiling. "Nancy Olton. You don't look like you're from New York."

Madison laughed, shifting her feet. "You'd be right."

Nancy snatched an empty box from the floor and started putting papers in it.

Why was she packing up everything?

"And no, he doesn't spend much time here, not when he can help it. But I can't blame him, what with the way his overbearing father runs this ship, trying to rule over everything Jake does." Nancy pushed her glasses farther up on her nose.

Jake had told her all about his domineering father and the ruthless way he managed things and she had said he had become like his father. What a far cry from the truth.

Seeing Colt Enterprises up close and in person, she understood more about Jake's life and the immense pressure he must have grown up in with all of this waiting for him to take over. It was the pressure he still lived with and the destiny that even now beckoned him. But he'd never bowed to that calling. He'd never bowed to any calling. Instead, he'd wandered from one thrill to the next.

Was his constant search for adventure an escape from all of this or was it what he really wanted in life?

Too many questions and none had answers until she could talk to Jake.

"Oh, great, speaking of. Just what I need right now," Nancy mumbled, shoving the box away with so much force a paperweight fell to the floor.

Madison turned around to see an older man with an uncanny resemblance to Jake barreling down on them. His face contorted in an angry glare and his arms pumped the air with every purposeful step he took, each one sending a loud thump reverberating around them. Not even the carpet could muffle the man's obvious rage. He could only be Jake's father.

He stormed up to the desk. "Olton, what could possibly be taking you so long to clear out of here? You were supposed to be gone hours ago. And where's my son? And who is this?" He indicated Madison with a disgusted glint in his eyes.

She stood tall. "I'm Madison Carmichael."

He reeled back with a sneer as if she might be contaminated, but recovered enough to lock his steel blue gaze on her. "Come to my office. We need to talk."

His tone indicated he would not be defied, but the red blotches on his face and the tight clenching of his fists told her it would be a bad idea.

She refused to give any sign of weakness. "No, thanks. I'm good here."

Shock crossed his face before morphing into pure fury.

"I can have security throw you out on your upstart, gold digging butt."

She raised her eyebrows. "That's okay because I was just about to leave."

She gave a quick nod to Nancy, who beamed at her with obvious pride and started to walk away.

"Is that it? You don't want to fight for your parents' winery or even ask me about the sale?" Clayton shouted.

She stopped, facing him head on. "That's not what I came here for."

Clayton sniggered. "If you came here for Jake, your chances were better with the winery. The boy's like me when it comes to women and we're not the commitment type. When he does marry, it'll be to someone with the appropriate background and connections, like his mother was."

A sickening sensation crawled through her stomach.

"That's right, little girl, you're outclassed. Jake's a big city type. He hates small towns almost as much as he hates me. But I have something he needs, something that will always keep him coming back. Money and this company. Blood will always be thicker than water. You didn't really think he'd stay with you in some hokey town, did you?"

His words echoed Tucker's to her so long ago, dismissing her with the same dagger-like efficiency, but she refused to give him the satisfaction of hurting her. These were his words not Jake's, and her worth had nothing to do with Clayton's opinion.

"You don't know the first thing about me." She kept her head high.

Clayton grunted. "Not worth my time."

He strode away down the hall, back to the elevators.

"Good for you, honey." Nancy stopped her efforts to pat Madison's shoulder. "Not many people stand up to him."

Madison relaxed her stance. "Thanks. What did he mean when you said you were supposed to clear out of here?"

"Just that. With Jake gone, I'm not about to stick around and play assistant to whatever executive pawn Clayton gets to replace him."

"Gone? What do you mean gone?" Madison stepped closer to the desk, tightening her grip on her bag.

Nancy lowered some cartons to the ground. "No longer with the company."

What did that mean? What was going on?

"Do you know where I can find Jake? I really need to see to him."

Now, more than ever.

Nancy studied her a moment before scribbling an address down on a piece of paper. "Here. This is the address for his apartment. Something tells me he wouldn't mind me giving it out to you."

"Thank you." She accepted the note.

"You should probably take these, too." Nancy handed her a small set of keys. "I'm not sure if he's there or not, and I wouldn't want you waiting out on the street or in the lobby."

"I appreciate all of your help." Madison tucked the keys in her bag and hurried to the elevators.

She managed to maneuver around the pedestrians zooming past her on the sidewalk and caught a cab. As the car jostled through the maze of streets with a steady stream of yellow traffic and blaring construction noises, she tried calling Jake. After a few rings, his voicemail picked up. She left him a brief message to let him know where to find her.

Jake had left Colt Enterprises. Why?

The obvious answer, that it had something to do with the sale of the winery, stood out to her, but why? And what did it mean for them?

Questions fought to burst out of her and she had no one to ask.

After paying the driver, she hitched her bag over her shoulder and stepped into the rich and polished lobby of Jake's apartment building.

She went up to the top floor. Of course, Jake had the penthouse. When she opened the door, an expansive, open floor plan met her. Everything shined, sparkled, and screamed expensive. It made Tucker's place look like a cheap knockoff. But this was Jake and things would go better this time. They had to; Jake meant so much more to her and with him, she would be willing to give up Serenity Creek and living close to her family. She could start her photography business all over again. But first she had to figure out his role in this whole convoluted sale situation.

Depositing her bag next to one of the modern couches, she took a seat, careful not to mess up anything. Images cycled through her mind of her and Jake. The way he made her bristle with a single word, the sense of protection he afforded her even when pulling her out of the ocean, the bliss that swept over her as he held her close on their moonlit stroll.

They all mingled together with more recent scenes. Jake's voicemail saying he'd left town, the phone conversation when she told him never to call her again, the smug look on his father's face when he looked down his nose at her.

Her phone buzzed and she knocked over her bag in her dash to grab it. "Hello."

"Maddy, it's Adam."

Her shoulders slumped. "Hey, Adam."

"How's it going over there?"

"Um, I'm not sure. I haven't seen Jake yet, but I have met his father, who told me straight out I'm from an inferior station in life."

"You're kidding, right?"

She sighed, exhaustion from the whole ordeal sneaking upon her. "I wish. Jake's not with Colt Enterprises anymore, and I don't know what that's all about. How are things at home?"

"That's why I'm calling. We found out who the new owner is. Madake Acquisitions."

"Who are they?"

"That's the problem. We can't find any information on them. They seem to be a new company. Mom and Dad are getting more than a little worried and, I have to admit, so am I."

"I don't blame them."

"Where are you?"

She took in Jake's home. "My own private Ritz Carlton."

"So you're at Jake's?"

"Yup."

"Where's he?"

"I don't know. I don't know anything right now," she admitted.

"Call me when you do."

She promised before nesting the phone in her lap, begging it to ring with Jake's name on the screen. Until then, she had nothing to do but wait.

# CHAPTER SEVENTEEN

The elevator dinged as Jake reached the floor of his office in Colt tower. Whistling, he strolled down the hallway. He had never considered marriage before, but now he was in the thick of it. The little jewelry bag he carried signaled just how far down the road he had gone. He only hoped Madison would join him.

He walked up to his secretary. "There's my favorite girl."

Nancy poked her head up from under the desk where she had been emptying drawers. Her eyeglasses stood slanted on her nose. "I doubt that. I'm twice your age and I've seen the women you go out with."

"None measure up to you." He hugged her.

She smiled up at him, her eyebrows raised. "Except one, maybe?"

He nodded, uncertain where her comment had come from. "Except one."

He stared down at the box holding framed pictures of her grown kids and grandkids. "It's not too late to come with me."

She shook her head. "No. I'm too old. I'm ready to retire and spend more time at home. You leaving is a great excuse for me to go as well."

"I can't thank you enough for all you've done for me. I wouldn't have survived this place without you."

She patted his cheek. The only woman he would ever allow to do such a thing, with the new exception of Rose who had also captured a special place in his heart.

"You've turned into a fine young man despite the brute of a father you have."

He pulled out a blue velvet box from the bag, slightly larger than the other box next to it. "This is for you."

She tsked. "You shouldn't have."

He loved watching the awe and appreciation spread across her face as she saw the emerald encrusted brooch in the shape of a lily, her favorite flower.

Her watery eyes met his. "Now I know why so many women fall at your feet. Come here, you."

She pulled him into her embrace.

"Not anymore." He chuckled. "I've become a permanent one woman guy. Off the market."

"Would that woman be blonde, pretty, down to earth, and have the heart of a lion?"

He rocked back on his heels, stunned by her words. Her description could be applied to only a single woman in his life. "Are you talking about Madison Carmichael? How did you know what she looks like? I thought I only told you about her over the phone."

She sighed, dropping into her chair. "She was here."

A jolt of electricity shocked his body, energizing every cell. She had flown to New York. For him. No small feat for a play it safe, keep everything in line woman with a fear of flying. She should never have had to tackle that fear or make such a choice. She had, though, and she'd picked him. They still had a chance and the ring nestled in the other velvet box would not be wasted. Relief flooded him like a shot of adrenaline.

"She was? When? Where is she now?" He paced in front of Nancy's desk, unable to keep still.

"About an hour ago. I sent her to your penthouse and gave her the spare keys I had."

"I have to go see her." He pivoted, desperate to get to her.

"Jake. There's more."

He stopped mid step, a chill slicing through his gut at the tone of her voice.

He faced her. "What happened?"

"Your father."

He clenched his jaw to keep from cursing in front of her.

She came around the desk to him. "Clayton got his fangs into her. Gave her that demeaning, you're-a-nobody look of his, and baited her with her parents' winery. Being that she didn't rise to the occasion, he went a step further and played the commitment card, saying you weren't into her or rural locations."

Raw rage coiled deep within him.

She raised her chin. "Madison carried herself real well, though. I haven't seen many people stand up to your father like that. She walked out of here with her head high and her dignity intact. You should have seen Clayton. I thought he was going to punch right through a wall and give himself a heart attack."

Pride swept through him. He shouldn't have expected anything less from his spitfire. His father's rude dismissal of her, though, made him seethe.

"Thank you for everything." He kissed her cheek, before stomping down the hallway.

"Wait. Where are you going?" she called after him.

He glanced over his shoulder. "To talk to my father for the last time, and then I have a hot date. At least I hope."

"Your mother would be awfully proud of you breaking off on your own, away from your father, and settling down. I hope you know that. She always wanted something different for you than what Clayton has."

He bowed his head, the warmth from the idea of his mom being pleased with his decision melting some of the frost that had overtaken him.

"Thanks, Nancy. That means a lot to me. More than you know. As do you." He gave her a final nod before making his way to the elevator.

He snatched the velvet box out of the bag and threw the bag in the trashcan, fingering the tiny case for a moment before stashing it in his pocket and checking his cell. One voicemail from Madison telling him she was at his penthouse. But before he talked to her, he had something he needed to take care of.

He rode to the top floor, wild fury flooding his veins. His body trembled with the effort of holding it back long enough to unleash it on Clayton and only Clayton.

The doors opened to a large, spacious room with uncomfortable, stiff backed chairs scattered next to the lengthy stretch of floor-to-ceiling windows on either side. The opulent room was meant to intimidate, and it had worked on him once, ages ago, but not now.

He stormed up to the huge, dark wood double doors leading to his father's office. The same pair that had terrified him as a child, irritated him when he was older, and irked him to no end in that moment.

Stomping into the room, he went right past his father's secretary.

"Wait, Mr. Colt. I haven't announced … Your father is … You know he doesn't like … "

Jake kept going, shoving open the doors of Clayton's inner domain. He threw them closed behind him with a loud whack, drowning out the secretary's pleas.

Clayton looked up from his imposing desk, a scowl imprinted on his face as he talked on the phone. "Sorry for the racket, Tom. No, it's nothing important."

Jake strode up to the desk, slamming his hands down and leaning over it. "We need to talk. Now."

Clayton waved him away. "What was that, Tom? I think so, too."

Jake snatched the phone in a single move. "He'll have to call you back."

Smashing the phone into the receiver, he glared at his father's face as red seeped into Clayton's skin.

"That was a very important call, boy, and I thought our business was done."

"I don't care if it was the President of the United States. I said I needed to talk to you. I thought we were done, too, until the stunt you pulled with Madison."

Clayton pushed back in his chair, folding his hands on his stomach. "Found out about that, did you? She come crying to you to save her from the big bad wolf?"

Jake ground his teeth.

"She's just playing you. Looking for a way to sink her teeth into all of our wealth."

"Enough." Jake smacked the desk. "She refused to give in to your bullying, and we both know it."

Clayton jabbed his finger in Jake's face. "Then why isn't she here with you? Because she ran away, didn't she?"

Heat pricked Jake's cheeks. "She chose not to descend to your street gutter level and took the high road."

Clayton spread his arms wide. "You can't be serious about this Carmichael girl. She's not from your world, Jake."

"You're not from my world."

Dark lines ground into Clayton's forehead. "I'm your father," he growled.

"Then act like it."

"What's that supposed to mean?"

"I love her. I thought I made that clear to you when I resigned. A father would want me to be happy, not drag me down."

"You can't be happy giving up a multi-million dollar inheritance and the chance to run this business all for some speck of a girl. You have no real chance together, especially with her parents' winery being sold under your watch."

Jake stared at him in silence, the ring burning a hole in his pocket.

Clayton seized on the opportunity. "You'll come over to my side soon enough. Once you see what it's like to live without cash and realize you've lost that girl for good."

"I'm going after her."

"Won't change anything."

"Yes, it will. I'm going to ask her to marry me."

Clayton surged to his feet. "You can't do that."

"I can and I will."

"That's the second dumbest thing you could ever do, next to resigning. What would a marriage to her bring you? Happy ever after is for fairytales, not the real world." Clayton's voice rose to a frenzy.

Jake kept his tone level. "It'll bring me something you never had. Love. And you no longer have a say in what I do. You never did and you never will."

Clayton huffed, taking a step back. "You always were difficult, never seeing reason." He shook his head. "I never should have sent you to that stupid winery. It did more harm than good. But it's sold and done with now. At least I made money on the deal. New owner paid a pretty penny more than that scrap of dirt was worth. And you can't turn your back on my company, on the wealth and power of our family name."

Jake looked him straight in the eye. "I turned my back on you a long time ago when Mom died, and you didn't even shed a tear or care about anything other than how it would affect you to have some kid around. I don't want your life, I want my own."

"You have no life. You gave it up the moment you turned in your resignation and I sold the winery. You lost your job and your precious girlfriend at the same time."

"I didn't lose the winery and I'm betting everything on the hope I didn't lose Madison."

Clayton rubbed his temple. "What are you talking about now?"

"I bought the winery."

Clayton's hand stilled as he aimed a menacing glare at him. "Excuse me?"

"I had my private lawyers set up a company name and handle the purchase for me so you wouldn't know I was behind it. I knew you would never sell it to me."

Clayton's whole body shook. He rounded the desk in an instant, stepping toe to toe with Jake. "You liar. You couldn't pull off a scheme like that, not in a million years, not on me. Where did you get the funds?" Spit spewed from his mouth as he shouted the question.

Jake never flinched. "I used the money Mom left me. I've never touched it until now. You were in such a hurry to dish out your revenge on me and so thrilled by the new dollar signs in front of you, you didn't even bother with your usual in-depth background checks."

Clayton stumbled back a step, a stunned expression soaking into his eyes, and something more. Something Jake could almost call pride. Could his father actually be proud of him under all that anger for taking such bold action and starting off on his own?

"You … you paid so much more than it was valued at," Clayton stammered.

"I would've paid anything to get that winery, and I knew a large figure would distract your attention."

"You would have upped your bid?"

"Yes. As it is I have a nice bundle left over. So while I'm not the wealthy king you are, I'm not a pauper either. And none of it matters. Money won't buy you what truly has worth."

Clayton slumped down into the guest chair, cradling his head in his hands.

Jake witnessed the defeat in the slope of his father's shoulders. An unexpected emotion overtook him: pity. Clayton invested everything in Colt Enterprises, in something that wouldn't outlive him and couldn't love him in return.

He touched his father's back. "I told you before that I didn't want to be here."

Clayton looked up at him. "I thought you were just young and naïve like some wild colt that had to be broken in. Who wouldn't want all of this?" He spread his arms to encompass his office.

"Me. The suit and tie deal isn't what I want. I've seen the backhanded way you handle things and it's not what I plan on doing. I need to work with my hands in the dirt. Specifically Carmichael dirt. You're going to keep your distance from Madison, her family, and me for a while. Don't try to contact me. I'll call you when I'm ready."

Clayton squinted up at him. "You think you can tell me what to do?"

"It's my turn."

"Who will take over when I'm gone?"

Jake sighed. "I don't know. Sell and retire if you like."

Clayton grunted.

"That's the problem, Clayton. You put too much into something that won't grow old with you. It'll just pass you by when you die. I plan to grow old with Madison if she'll still have me."

"You're really going through with this?"

Jake nodded. "Goodbye."

He started toward the door, but Clayton's voice, barely above a whisper stopped him.

"Jake."

He turned around.

"Will I see you again?"

For the first time, Jake saw real fear in his father's countenance.

"Of course. I'd like for us to be the father and son we've never been someday. I don't want to forget the only dad I've ever known."

A frail, weak version of Clayton smiled back at him, an image of the path he could have taken. He could have lived hard like him, all business and currency. He'd chosen the better road with

Madison and some grapevines. All he had to do was convince her to take a chance and wear the ring in his pocket.

"I'll be in touch, Clayton. Later. Much later. Right now, I have someone waiting for me."

He strode from the room, shutting the door behind him with a resounding click and moving forward with a renewed hope.

# CHAPTER EIGHTEEN

Madison stared into the abyss of her sizeable, incredibly strong coffee as if it held the answers to the unknowns cycling through her mind. Taking a long drink, she reveled in the rich flavor and sorely needed energy boost. It had taken thirty minutes to figure out Jake's high tech coffee contraption, but the first sip alone was worth it. If she ended up living here, at least the coffee would be good. And she'd be with Jake.

A click sounded through the empty apartment, followed by footsteps.

She didn't consider her actions, just ran straight for Jake.

All the questions, the problems, the obstacles that had loomed so large before her fell. Right then only Jake mattered. Reaching him, touching him, kissing him.

She charged up to him, throwing herself into his arms.

Jake caught her with a chuckle, holding her tightly against him. Cradling her neck, he kissed her soft and sweet.

He pulled his head up, keeping his arms around her.

"What's going on? Who's the new owner of Oak Hills? Do you know him?" She had meant to say she loved him and he should never leave without her again, but the words got bogged down by the confusion engulfing her.

He grinned. "Very well, actually."

What all had he kept from her?

Her stomach sank and she pulled back from his grasp, but he tightened his grip.

She squinted at him. "Well, who is this mystery person, then? Why did you leave without telling me about your father selling the winery? Why did you quit?"

He laughed. Flat out laughed, making her simmering blood boil.

She struggled against his hold on her. "I don't see what's so funny."

"Easy there, spitfire. Let me start with your first question. I'm the new owner."

She halted her attempts at wrestling free of his embrace, blinking blindly up at him. "Excuse me? I'm lost already. Can you back up a couple of steps? You're the new owner?"

He lowered his hands to intertwine them with hers. "My father wanted to turn the winery into a hotel. I couldn't let Oak Hills be demolished. I know what that would do to you and your family. I had to move quickly, and that meant collaborating with my lawyers to set up a company my father wouldn't recognize so I could buy the winery with the money my mother left me."

"Why didn't you tell me?"

"It all happened so fast, I didn't have time, and I didn't know what to say to you until I had a better hold of the situation. Once I did, I tried explaining things to you, that night on the phone."

She cringed. "I'm sorry, I shouldn't have said that about you being like your father and I should have listened to you. You know you didn't have to handle this alone. I could have helped you. You could have told me up front. Even if it was in a voicemail." She stepped closer, staring up at him.

"You're right and I should have."

"So Madake Acquisitions is you?"

He squeezed her hands. "It's us."

Understanding dawned on her. Madake. A melding of their names. Madison and Jake. He had been thinking of them this whole time. Of what mattered to her. Warmth seeped through her from her head to her toes.

"Is that why you resigned?"

"Yes. I want to make a new life. With you."

Love, fresh and fierce, burst within her heart. "What does that mean for us, exactly?"

"You're the only woman I've thought of settling down with. You're the only one I've ever considered proposing to and you'd better be the last."

She launched herself against him, kissing him and giggling all the while. "That's good, really good, because I love you and I found out my life doesn't work without you. Not my photography, not my business, nothing is the same without you. I need you. I … wait, did you say propose?"

He chuckled, circling his fingers around her wrists and removing her hands from his neck to drop down on one knee.

She gasped, a tremble of joy vibrating through her.

He took her left hand. "Madison, I love you. With all my heart. With all my soul. I can't imagine a future without you. I want to grow old with you, with kids, grandkids, the whole package. You're home. My home." He pulled a small velvet box out of his pocket. "Apparently, when you came to my office, I was out buying a very important piece of jewelry."

He opened the box to reveal a sparkling pear shaped diamond solitaire. "Will you marry me?"

Fresh tears marred her vision as she nodded.

"Yes," she whispered and, finding her voice, spoke it louder, "Yes."

He rose to his feet, gathering her in his arms, and sinking his face into hair. Twirling her around, he kissed her lips, her cheeks, her temple, every part of her face.

"Yes, yes, yes," she repeated, laughing under the rainfall of his kisses as the apartment spun around her.

But she kept her gaze steady, set on a single entity. Jake.

He set her feet on the ground, slipping the ring onto her finger. "I love you, Madison Carmichael."

He rested his forehead against hers.

"I love you, Jake Colt."

Gazing up at him, she took in every inch of their picture perfect moment. Together.

"I have one more question for you."

"Name it," he whispered.

"Where are we going to live?"

He grinned. "I'll show you."

• • •

Madison watched as Jake lifted his MD 600N into the air, noting the ease with which he handled the controls next to her and told herself the dips and vibrations were normal.

Her stomach plummeted as they climbed into the air. "I can't believe you actually got me up in this thing."

"I told you I would show you where we're going to live." His voice sounded garbled through her headset even though he sat right next to her, but that had more to do with the blood thundering in her ears than the blades churning above them.

"I didn't think you meant literally. And from the air no less."

"If you can fly to New York, you can fly in a helicopter."

"It's a little different when you actually see everything ahead of and beneath you."

"Better?"

She gazed out the window as they soared through the air. Greens, browns, and blues flashed before her as they flew over fields, forests, and neared the creek. The roaring noise settled to a purr as her blood pressure calmed down.

"Kind of. More terrifying, but beautiful."

He chuckled. "The terror part should subside soon."

"You have high hopes."

"In you, always."

"Do you always know the right thing to say? I mean does it come naturally or something?"

"Sometimes. Other times I have to work at it, but it's worth it." He winked at her.

She smiled, sinking back into the seat with a thump.

"There's Twin Oaks Farm." He pointed off to the right.

She caught a quick sight of horses grazing. To think she'd ridden one of those with Jake and now here she was flying next to him with his ring on her finger. The simple diamond twinkled up at her in the sunlight.

"And there's Oak Hills." He pointed to the winery.

She leaned forward. "That's where you landed."

The exact spot that had set her on an uncharted course.

"That it is." He flew over the property. "You've shown me what I want to do, and it means staying right here, working the vineyard with your dad, and sharing everything together. You and me. Do you think your dad will mind having me be more hands on with the wines? I know how bothersome those new owners can be, but I thought I might get some grace with his daughter being my new partner and all."

Absolute joy wrapped around her. "I can't think of a better beginning for us."

She took in the view as they glided over the oak trees, Victorian spires, and vineyards she knew so well. This was their time. Their present and their fearless future.

# ABOUT THE AUTHOR

Kate Kadence lives on the California Coast where she loves to write and enjoy beautiful sunsets with her family. You can learn more about her and her works in progress at *www.KateKadence.com*.

# A Sneak Peek from Crimson Romance
## (From *Hiding Places* by Ellen Parker)

"He's coming after you, sis."

Mona Smith tensed and straightened her spine to parallel the gray metal chair. Matt's voice grated harsh on her ears as he slowed his words through a split lip. *Who beat you?* She focused on her brother's face, remembering him without a black eye and dark bruises against prison orange clothing.

The clink of metal against metal caused her to glance around the plain gray room. Three other tables of inmates, confined with shackles, and their visitors talked under the watchful gaze of a uniformed Minnesota Department of Corrections officer near the door. She made a quick comparison to last week's visit at the county jail and didn't like the difference. She breathed in a little courage. If Matt could live here for two years, she would visit. After all, she was the dependable child, the big sister attempting to keep little brother out of trouble.

"Who?" She rested her palms on the table, careful not to touch her brother.

"Basil. My boss. You've met him."

She nodded as a cold shiver crossed her shoulders. Basil Berg embodied pure trouble. Matt had pointed him out months ago with a warning not to get involved. From what Mona picked up from stray bits of conversation, Basil's primary revenue source was party drugs. Prostitution and burglary rounded out his business. "He came into the diner twice last week."

"Not good, sis."

"He behaves as a customer. No reason to refuse service." He also drank iced tea with a full breakfast at three in the morning and stared at her past polite intervals. She felt like a mouse dropped into a snake's cage when he looked her direction. "Why is he coming after me?"

Matt glanced toward the guard before dropping his voice even lower. "Money. Twenty-five grand."

"That's a year's wages. I don't have that sort of cash." Cool moisture gathered on Mona's neck. She separated her hands to reach for a tissue before realizing her pockets were empty. The only possession the officials let her bring into this room was a bright orange key to the locker in the reception area. "If I did—"

"I know." Matt lifted one slight shoulder. "You'd pay off Mother's final medical bills."

"It's the honest thing to do." She sealed her lips before the beginning of their late mother's basic monologue on the advantage of truth over expediency slipped out. She'd be visiting her brother at a Minneapolis park or coffee shop instead of prison if he'd taken that advice. "How did Basil get the notion I have money?"

Matt rubbed the three stars tattooed on his right forearm. "He got bad information. One of his minions convinced him I withheld a portion of his take on the pawnshop heist. I didn't. Always gave him his cut on assignments."

"Then—"

"I freelanced. A few jobs. Small stuff. Neighbor of the old lady they accused me of assaulting. One or two profitable break-ins the week before. You don't need the details." Matt dipped his face to rub one ear with a manacled hand. "Didn't get near the amount his imaginative lackey reported. But Basil's prone to believe what he wants."

"He gives me the creeps." *And watches me like a predator.* "Should I call the police if I see that flashy ride of his near the apartment?"

"No." Matt jerked back, his chains clattering against the metal table, and the guard gave them a hard look. He eased forward again and lowered his voice to soft conversation volume. "Don't call the cops on Basil—ever. And for your information, he drives a restored El Camino."

She studied his face, and rated the expression as panic level twelve on a scale of ten. "Why shouldn't I call the cops on him?"

"You'd have another funeral to arrange. I didn't walk into a door." He pointed first to his face and then to several bruises along the edge of his prison clothes. "Initiation. All I did was walk across the yard. Basil's inside men play rough."

"I'm leaving the apartment in two weeks." She paused for an instant. Would his next sentence change her plans again? Her friend offered cheap rent but she didn't want to put another person in danger. "I'm moving in—"

"Don't tell me." A shake of his head reinforced his words. "Don't tell anyone. Just do it."

"It's that bad?" Mona rubbed her thumbs in lieu of asking the questions popping up like poisonous mushrooms after a rain. How much was Basil capable of? Could he order a murder to occur inside prison? Like a movie? She refused to put Matt's life at further risk. The two of them only had each other. She chose not to count Aunt Lucy in Duluth. Mother's sister was nice, she'd even helped with the funeral expenses, but their bond with her didn't run deep.

"You know what to do."

She nodded. Through the years they'd discussed several ways Matt could leave the Twin Cities and start fresh. Half of them involved a vanishing act before looking up their father. It'd been three years since the last letter from Joseph Ignatius Smith. She closed her eyes and thought hard for a moment, but the name of the city in Washington State on the envelope didn't come. In all their bantered planning through the years she'd never thought she'd be the one needing to run. "I don't want to abandon you."

"I'm past your help. You need to take care of you." He leaned forward to the invisible midline of the table.

She sighed. Matt was right. She needed to get away, give Basil and his drug organization time to forget her. *I'll start when I get home.* A list of actions to take, beginning with giving notice and asking for a reference at the diner, had already started in the list-making portion of her mind. She'd find a place to land and seek work. She could waitress. Or cook. Or work as a maid.

"Two minutes, visitors." The guard announced the imminent end of their time together.

"Until next time?" Matt looked up from his handcuffs and stared into her eyes.

"Yes. Next time." She struggled with the lump in her throat representing how long to "next time." Would it be weeks? Months? When she walked out of this windowless room and back into an early June afternoon, would it be up to Matt to find her after his two-year sentence? She stared into his deep, dark eyes and memorized the face too worn for twenty-three years. "Take care, little brother."

• • •

Mona opened the brass mailbox and tucked the contents into her waistband. A moment later she unlocked the apartment building's interior door and headed for the stairs. Bits and pieces of Matt's conversation continued to chase each other, undeterred by the three bus transfers, two-block walk, and pleasant spring weather.

*Will I visit the prison again?* She grasped the wooden handrail at memory of all the negative aspects of the visit. Even after researching the facility, the sheer size had nearly overwhelmed her. She'd expected rules and formality, but not the extent of the difference with the county jail.

*He's coming after you. Initiation.* Matt's words, plus the tone of voice used to say them, were enough to keep a person awake at night. Her self-assigned duty to protect Matt needed to be put on hold. He told her to take care of herself. The best way to be the good big sister in this case was to get away from Basil's reach.

She paused, adjusted a backpack strap, and listened to the soft thud of the elevator doors half a flight above her. The elderly motor started, hesitated, and began again with a steady growl. Even after three years in this building the sound still brought thoughts of a tiger staking claim to supper. She continued her climb to the third floor.

A few moments later Mona tensed in front of her apartment. The door, so carefully closed and locked behind her this morning, showed a sliver of air between the frame and panel. She threaded her keys between the fingers of her right hand and nudged the door open with her foot.

Silence. And—smoke? A cigar? She eased inside and stifled a gasp. Drawers and their contents lay scattered across the living room floor. The closet door stood open, the boxes from the shelf strewn on the carpet. To her left, the Murphy bed doors were flung wide, the bed pulled a third of the way down like a monster emerging from the wall.

*He's coming after you.* For an instant the room sucked her into a gray whirlpool. She sagged, rested one shoulder against the wall, and wrapped her arms in a self-hug. Basil carried cigars. He'd been here—moments ago. Had she avoided him only by taking the stairs? She concentrated on taking her next breath.

The plans for her disappearance tomorrow, plotted during the long bus ride, vanished. She needed to go. Now. Forget giving notice at work. Jennifer, her best friend, would have to cope without a phone call.

Mona hurried to the bedroom and began to fill her backpack. She picked up enough clean clothes from the confusion in front of the dresser to last a few days. Documents and papers from one of the drawers lay across the bed and she gathered two large handfuls, stuffed them under her best jeans in the backpack, and added today's mail to the stash. In the bathroom she grabbed only her toothbrush and small cosmetic case. *Money.* She carried seventeen dollars and a transit card in her pockets. Not enough.

She took her full pack across the defiled living room and dropped it beside a tipped dinette chair. Both hands swept up to block her mouth as her foot touched the kitchen vinyl. *I will not scream.* She forced her gaze to move across the kitchen from top to bottom, left to right. Every cabinet door hung open. Flatware, broken china, and kitchen gadgets lay on every flat surface. A tipped bottle of olive oil dripped into a mound of rice on the floor.

One step forward, then another, she forced her body to move until she stood by the sink. In the photo she stood, smiling, at the diner's cashier station. Now the picture was fastened to a thick cutting board with her best boning knife, the tip through the base of her throat. Red marker repeated the threat: "I'm coming."

She reached back, pulled out her phone, and flipped it open. Her fingers dialed without an order from her brain.

"Emergency services. May I help you?"

"Uh." She gripped the phone and sealed her lips. Matt. *Never call the police on Basil.* She couldn't put his life at greater risk. He was all her family that mattered. "No. I'm sorry. It's been a mistake."

She snapped the phone shut and tossed it into the trash.

Within two minutes she'd retrieved the cloth bag of cash from the never-used electric teakettle. By rare good luck it had escaped notice in the back of a base cabinet. On her way to the door she added her Chinese grandparents' wedding photo, cracked glass and all, plus the framed portrait of her mother to her luggage. She settled the backpack on her shoulders and snatched a pastel blue ball cap and her windbreaker from the closet floor. In the doorway she turned for a final look and blew a kiss to the apartment of memories.

"Fastest way out of town." She muttered her need as she hurried down three flights of stairs. She discarded the idea of the bus; during the wait at the Greyhound station she'd be a target. She needed something quick and private. She exited the apartment building and turned away from her usual bus stop. Six blocks away she could catch a train at the light rail platform. From there—

She crossed the first side street, and hurried her steps. At the next cross street she tensed at a glimpse of bright red paint and polished chrome. She blinked, confirmed it was Basil's restored classic El Camino, and pulled in a deep breath.

*Walk. Don't run or act guilty.* Mona crushed her windbreaker against her chest and marched toward the light rail stop.

In the mood for more Crimson Romance?
Check out *Waking Up to Love* by Evan Purcell at
*CrimsonRomance.com.*